BLOWN AWAY

AND OTHER STORIES

L P FERGUSSON

Cover artwork: LP Fergusson

To my very own Max Black

Created with Vellum

CONTENTS

ABOUT THE AUTHOR

LP Fergusson is a writer based in Oxfordshire. She has an MA in Creative Writing from Oxford Brookes University and won the Blackwell's Prize in 2015. In 2020 she was a Historical Writers Association Gold Crown judge. She is also the editor of the blog *With Love from Graz,* which was featured on BBC Radio Wales, Radio 2 and the BBC4 programme *A Very British Romance* with Lucy Worsley. Her psychological thriller *The Fever Box* won Fictionary's Book of the Year 2022. As LP Fergusson she writes historical fiction, *A Dangerous Act of Kindness* (2019) is set in a rural community in 1940, and *The Summer Fields* which focusses on the Battle of Blenheim, and as Loraine Fergusson she writes a series of cosy mysteries set in Duntisbourne Hall, a rundown stately home on the borders of Wales. Blown Away went on to inspire a scene in The Hipkiss File, the most recent in the series.

Website: https://lpfergusson.com/

INTRODUCTION

My writing career took off in later life, starting with an MA in Creative Writing from Oxford Brookes University. As a new writer, getting noticed is vital. Along with submitting endless first chapters and synopses, online competitions seemed a great way to get my name out there – Bridport or BBC Short Story winners caught the eye of agents and publishers, whilst other competitions had agents on the judging panel who may, just may, ask to see something more. If you made the longlist or the shortlist, you could put it on your cv as an indication that you know what you're doing as a writer.

As I worked on my full-length novel, I submitted short fiction to every outlet I could find. I didn't think much about the entry fee – sometimes it cost me nothing, other times I paid anything from £8 to an eye-watering €20. Some offered feedback, but only if you payed extra for it (Fish Publishing charge €55 on top of the entry fee). By the end of the first year, I totted up how much I'd spent – it was nearly £800 to achieve two longlist and one shortlist place. I was horrified.

I understand that there is a cost to running a writing

competition, but I'm troubled that so many are unregulated. Chatting to writer friends who have been asked to judge competitions, it's generally for glory, not money, and I've come across some terrible stories – judges not bothering to read all the entries, prestigious authors setting up a competition, but never paying out the prize pot. Mostly it's a story of trusting writers paying the entry fee in the forlorn hope that their story will be read. I resolved to be more careful.

I discovered NYC Midnight in 2018. It's a knockout competition, kicking off in January with an assignment giving you a genre, subject and character. You have eight days to write 2,500 words. If your story is one of the top five in your group, you get a new assignment and three days to write up to 2000 words. Round 3, new assignment and two days for 1,500 words, and the finalists get a new assignment and a mere 24 hours to write 1,250.

I was excited by the format. It was pricey compared to other competitions, but worth every penny because of the feedback. Astonishingly, every single writer receives feedback (and this year that was well over five thousand writers). The judges are perceptive, encouraging, thorough and inspiring (you can read an example of their feedback on one of my stories here). I've entered every year since, made it through to Round 2 each year, and Round 3 twice. It's resulted in a lot of stories, and here they are.

The assignment prompts are fun too. If you want to have a go yourself, you can find the list of the challenges I've written for here before you read my story and see what you come up with.

BLOWN AWAY

Genre: Comedy • **Theme**: An exchange of gifts • **Character**: A nosy neighbour

Two old chums, returning from a boozy night out together, get into a heap of trouble on the riverbank.

Marvellous way to travel, BS Moreton thought, hunkering down into the collar of his winter coat. Major Frodsham leant nonchalantly on the tiller of Blown Away, his rheumy eyes eagerly scanning the dark river ahead. The temperature had dropped considerably since earlier in the evening and a cold breeze was blowing off the water, but BS felt warm as toast. The Blue Acorn had laid on a fantastic dinner and the two old chums had imbibed sufficient alcohol to keep the chills at bay. An intoxicating sense of freedom filled BS's veins and he gave a spontaneous bark of laughter.

"Patricia thinks I'm in Leominster," he said.

"Doing what?"

"Seeing our daughter."

"Isn't that a bit risky, old chap? You should have fessed up and said you were spending an evening with me."

"She doesn't trust you, Frodders. She thinks you'll lead me astray." Frodders nodded sagely, but he didn't contradict him. "It's the last proper drink I'll have until the two of us meet up again in the New Year," BS added gloomily.

"Surely Patricia doesn't ban the odd snifter over the festivities, does she?"

"I'm very much afraid she does. And let me tell you, Frodders, Christmas is a cheerless prospect without a drink to see you through."

"No wonder you get so chap-fallen at this time of year. Shame we can't round off tonight with a quick nightcap, but we've drunk everything on board."

"What? You can't be serious. You drink like a fish, Frodders."

Frodders pursed his lips together and pretended he was blowing bubbles. It was very funny.

"Honestly, Frodders, you can be an ass," BS said. "Besides, we haven't finished everything," and he reached under the seat and drew out a decidedly bottle-shaped present, rather badly wrapped. Frodders bent stiffly forward and gave the paper an exploratory squeeze.

"That feels awfully like a bottle of port," he said appreciatively. He returned to the tiller and looked down at BS with a jovial anxiety. "We never swap presents at Christmas," he said. "I haven't got a thing for you."

"It's not really a Christmas present," BS said. "It's a thank you for taking me up river to the pub and then giving me a berth for the night so that I could enjoy that very good bottle of Shiraz with my dinner."

"Bottles," Frodders said, emphasising the plural with a

snigger.

"Well, that vintage did rather spank the palate. It would have been a shame to stop at one."

"The very best thing to have with port," Frodders said, "is a hearty cheese."

"I'm not meant to have that either."

"Well, that's a blessing – because I haven't got any." They both began to laugh.

"I like nuts with my port," BS said.

"Nuts to you, then." That also seemed awfully funny. "I haven't got any nuts either,' Frodders said.

"Really, old chap? It doesn't show," and they were off again.

By the time Frodders had wiped the tears from his eyes and BS had given his nose a mighty blow, the moon had emerged from behind a strip of cloud, turning the river into quicksilver, the reflections dancing ahead of them.

"Time for radio silence," Frodders said quietly, pointing ahead to where the other narrowboats were moored along the bank, their lights dropping in ribbons onto the black body of moving water. "I'll moor upstream of Miss Crow's boat. That woman is quite unable to keep her nose out of other people's business. If she spots us, she'll be off her boat and onto the bank like a trap door spider and in next to no time the whole town will know we've both got a bit squiffy."

"The whole town? That's a bit of an exaggeration, old chap."

Frodders gave a puff of derision and said, "I kid you not – and first on her list will be your wife, Patricia."

"Dear God! Do you think so? That would really put the cat among the pigeons. I'd better go below and douse the lights."

Frodders raised a gloved thumb and nodded, adding in a stage whisper, "There's a mooring about a hundred yards up ahead. We'll pull in there for the night but you're going to have to get out onto the bank and tie the boat up."

"I'm going forward," BS said importantly.

He maneuvered himself down through the rear hatch with a grunt, navigating the length of the boat in a stoop, his hands on either wall to steady himself. Blown Away was a neat little vessel, only twenty-five feet long with a flat hull and four hopper windows, two on each side. Frodders cut the engines and the sound of the water slapping against the hull filled the silence. BS switched off the lights, leaving only the glow from the wood-burning stove to illuminate the interior.

By the time he remerged on the tiny bow deck, Frodders was expertly bringing the narrowboat in parallel to the bank.

"It's a bit unsteady," BS said, bumping back and forth as he tried to keep his balance.

"Keep your voice down," Frodders hissed over the low roof. "I'll bring her in close. All you have to do is step off."

"That's easy for you to say. I'm not the man I used to be."

"Would you rather take the tiller?"

BS gave Frodders a sour look but he probably didn't see it in the dark. "No," he said.

"Pick up the rope then. You can see the bollard up ahead. Here it comes. Get ready."

BS put a foot up on the gunwale and grabbed hold of the roof of the cabin. The side of the boat gently skimmed the bank, the long grass hissing against the hull. "Now," Frodders whispered urgently.

BS stepped up and his gammy knee gave way. He tipped forwards. He fumbled for a handhold and felt the aluminum of the roof slither beneath his palm before shooting his hand into fresh air. Over he went, landing face down on the bank with a dreadful expulsion of air.

"Ruddy hell!" he heard Frodders say. "The rope, man.

Keep hold of the rope."

BS didn't have much choice. It was wrapped firmly round his wrist and tightening. He felt his arm extending and slowly, inexorably, his body began to move through the grass.

"What are you doing?" Frodders hissed.

BS couldn't answer. The boat was pulling him gently forward on his front and he had a facefull of grass. He felt a stick lodge against his right ear. As the weight of the boat dragged him slowly forward, the stick began to dig in. He tried to reach it with his free hand. Just when he thought it was about to cleave his outer ear in two, it broke with a sharp snap. The slope of the bank rotated him slowly over again and he looked up at a sky full of dizzying stars.

"The bollard's there man. On your right-hand side," Frodders said, his voice no longer a whisper but cracking with anger and panic. "You're right on top of it."

"You're dragging me," BS moaned.

"I can't stop the boat unless you get the rope round the bollard."

"Help me," BS said. Slowly, inexorably he was rolled onto his front again. It felt as if his shoulder was dislocating. Everything moved in an agony of slow motion. Lifting his head, he could see the dark shape of the bollard up ahead, but he'd also spotted a large pebble just in front of him. Unable to avoid it, the pebble disappeared under his armpit. His body rose over it and it bulged painfully under his sternum before inching its way under his generous belly. He felt his skin puckering around it. And pop! It flew out sideways, landing in the water with a splash.

"The bollard's by your head. Reach out, man."

"I'm slipping down the bank."

"Reach out.'

'I can't."

"It's there."

The bollard, hard and immovable, pressed onto his scalp. His head came to a halt. The rest of his body didn't. The bollard settled against his neck. Spread-eagled, his legs moved round like the hands of giant clock, as the rope dragged him on and on.

"For the love of God," Frodders said. "You've missed it."

"Help!"

"There's another one in ten yards. It's our last chance."

Silently, BS submitted to his fate. Mud seeped through the knees of his trousers, his nostrils filled with the smell of damp earth and riverweed. Any minute now, he thought, my face will be dragged through something a great deal worse. How he rued the days when he only pretended to pick up after the dog, scooping a clean pebble into the doggie dirt bag to fool the other dog walkers that he was doing his civic duty.

The bank sloped nearer to the water. The hull of the boat towered above his prone body. Frodder's voice drifted down from the deck above, "It's coming up now. If you miss this one, we'll plough right into Miss Crow's boat."

Panting, BS made another supreme effort to lift his head. He could just make out the second bollard ahead, a stout lump of blackened metal. He reached forward with his other hand, grabbing at the rope. As the bollard neared, he pushed his knees into the soft earth, raising up just enough to throw the rope around before the weight of the boat pulled it taut.

He sat back, unwinding the rope from his arm and giving his poor, bruised wrist a rub. He heard a hiss of friction next to him. Holy Mary Mother of God! The rope was slipping off. He threw himself onto the wriggling snake, lashed it round the bollard, once, twice. He breathed a great sigh of relief.

"The stern! The stern!" Frodders shouted, alarming a couple of ducks that quacked angrily as they fled, their wing clapping the water. The bow of the boat was secured, but the back, caught by the current, was swinging gently out into the river. "Get up! I'll throw you a rope."

Bloody hell, BS thought. I'm exhausted. He struggled to his feet and plodded miserably up the towpath. A coil of rope flew out of the darkness and him sharply across the face.

"Blow me down to the ruddy ground," BS muttered to himself. "That's a hell of way to say thank you."

He stamped around in the grass, desperately trying to find the rope. There was a hollow thud out in the river followed by a none-too-pleasant expletive from his friend and all of a sudden, the bank was flooded with light, pouring from the open door of a moored narrowboat.

"What on earth are you doing?" Miss Crow said.

"Bumping into your boat," BS replied benignly. He could now see the rope on the ground and bent stiffly to retrieve it. "Must secure the back of the boat," he called, limping off down the bank, principally to get a good angle on the rope to haul in the stern, but also to get downwind of Miss Crow. He must smell like a barmaid's apron.

To his great relief, he saw her disappear into the bowels of her boat. He hauled on the rope and slowly, inexorably the silhouette of Frodders, standing in the stern with arms raised in frustrated disbelief, came towards him.

"You blithering idiot," Frodders said once he was in earshot. "You made a right pig's breakfast of that – and she caught you, red-handed."

"But I think we're all right," BS said as he lashed the rope around the bollard. "She's gone back inside."

"Quick," Frodders said, "Get on board. We must batten down the hatches, we must..."

"Helloo! Major!" a shrill voice called and to BS's horror, he saw Miss Crow trotting down the towpath towards them, waving something above her head.

"Pull me in, Frodders," BS said and, as his friend hauled him over the gunwale, his foot struck something on the floor of the boat and he stumbled, tumbling into Frodders with a groan. "The bottle," he said. "It's rolling around on the deck. Grab it Frodders. She's nearly here."

Frodders felt around the deck with his hands. "I've got it," he said, holding it up triumphantly. "Howzat!" he cried.

'Oh, Major Frodsham," a voice from the bank said. "You complete darling. And I've got a little something for you too," and before either of the men could move, Miss Crow leant into the boat, pressed a wrapped package into Frodders' other hand and swept BS's present into her own. "You really shouldn't have," she said joyfully. "You are the best neighbor a dull old spinster like myself could wish for. Happy Christmas!" and she was gone.

"Well, blow me down to the ruddy ground," BS said. "She's taken my present."

Frodders, who was once again giving a good impression of a fish, stared at the retreating figure. "I think we may have got away with it," he said. "Come on. Quick. Before she comes back."

They clattered down into the cabin, shut and bolted the door and sank down on the narrow berth, still panting from their exertions. "That was close," Frodders said with a sigh.

"But the port. She's taken the port. There goes our nightcap."

"I'm not so sure," Frodders said. "This feels decidedly bottle-shaped," and in the half-light of the stove, he raised a hopeful eyebrow at BS, his eyes gleaming. "Shall we have a look?"

"Open it before Christmas?"

"Why not?"

With feverish excitement Frodders began to pull at the ribbon.

"A nice bottle of whiskey, perhaps?" BS said.

"A cheeky little brandy?" Frodders speculated.

"It's dark green," BS said as the paper fell away.

"Burgundy!" Frodders said, but then he went completely still, staring down at the label. "It's handwritten," he said in an ominous tone.

"What?"

"The label – it's ruddy well handwritten." He got stiffly to his feet and hobbled over to the stove, holding the label towards the glow coming from the embers.

"What does it say?" BS asked, his voice full of anxiety.

"Hedgerow wine," Frodders said.

"Holy Mary Mother of God! You can't be serious."

Frodders sank back onto the berth, his shoulders slumped. He sighed heavily and said, "We may as well give it a go."

A LITTLE WHILE LATER, BS held his glass to the light. "It's awfully green," he said.

"How bad can it be?" Frodders said.

BS raised it to his lips. It smelt of burnt match and wet dog with a hint of skunk. He took a tentative sip – wet straw, a slap of ethyl acetate and the bitter finish of artificial sweetener.

"Good grief," BS said, his face twisting into a terrible grimace. "If that doesn't make a fellow take the pledge, nothing will."

Frodders eyed his own glass suspiciously before saying, "Oh, well – in for a penny and all that. Happy Christmas."

FIRST PLACE in category

THE SHIVERING LADDER

Genre: Ghost Story • **Theme:** A silent auction • **Character:** A loiterer

A mistake at a charity auction has terrifying consequences for an Oxford don.

The lights along Oxford's High glittered gamely through the fog, gusts of laughter bursting from the bars along the way. Just before he turned off into Queen's Lane, a young woman called out, "Merry Christmas, Prof," and he returned the greeting cheerfully. He didn't recognise her, but all the students in Oxford knew him by sight, with his mane of white hair, his saturnine dark eyebrows and his attentive gaze.

The chill air of the night seemed concentrated in this cobbled alley. The Prof tugged the collar of his coat higher and pushed his hands deeper into his pockets. He smiled as his fingers made contact with the small wooden box, his only acquisition from this evening's charity event.

When he reached the door of Mordiford College, he thought he saw a figure hanging around the top of Queen's Lane, but when he peered, the shadow seemed to melt into the mist. He pushed open the heavy front door and called out a cheery, "Good evening, Ron," as he passed the porter's lodge. A nuggety little man looked out and replied with some urgency, "Professor Cartwright. There's a call in here for you."

The Prof slowed. "Put it through to my rooms. I'll take it up there."

But Ron had already opened the lodge door and stood, silhouetted against the light, the phone's receiver in his hand. "It's the Pitt Rivers Museum."

"Pitt Rivers? But I've just come from there."

Ron waggled the receiver in his direction, nodding urgent encouragement. With a sigh, the Prof complied. The heat inside the lodge engulfed him, instantly misting up his spectacles. He took the phone.

"Professor Cartwright? It's Els van der Berg." The Prof knew the director of the museum by reputation, but they had never been introduced. "I'm sorry to disturb you at this late hour, but we have a rather embarrassing situation." Intriguingly, there was a touch of humour in her tone. "The meeting room where the silent auction was organised this evening had been used earlier in the day to unpack some items sent over from the Commonwealth Museum in Boston. Unfortunately, the auction organisers arrived a little early to set up, and somehow one of the fundraisers mistook an artifact as a donation, and put it on display."

The Prof pulled the box from his pocket, turning it in his hand. "It wasn't a rather crude piece of folk art by any chance, was it?"

"I'm very much afraid that it was." He could hear by her voice that she was smiling. "And yours was the winning bid."

"The only bid, as I recall." The Prof began to chuckle. He gave an amused shrug towards Ron. "I suppose you want it back?"

"I do. The organisers will reimburse you, naturally…"

"I wouldn't dream of it. It was only a few pounds. They were raising money for a good cause."

"That's extremely decent of you. I shall send someone over to Mordiford College tomorrow to collect it."

There was something in the lightness of her tone, the humour in her voice, an attractive timbre of accent that he couldn't quite place that made him eager to put a face to the voice. "Not at all. You're only fifteen minutes' walk from here. Let me return it to you in the morning. You are open on Christmas Eve."

The Prof was still laughing when he handed Ron the phone and explained what had happened.

"Never heard of a silent auction," Ron said.

"It's a new thing. American I expect, but an enjoyable evening."

Ron glanced down at the box. "I wouldn't pay fifty pence for that."

"Oh, I don't know – I found it rather intriguing." He checked his watch. "Is the Senior Common Room open. I fancy a nightcap before turning in."

"I'll come and unlock for you, sir," Ron said, pulling on his overcoat and taking a set of keys from the panel.

As they left the welcome glow of the lodge and walked through to Back Quad, the shouts of the revellers out in the streets floated over the roofs. In the cloisters the dismal weather of the past few days seemed colder still, as if the mist that crept along the ground was oozing from the stones themselves. The moisture in the air chilled the Prof's face and glistened on the cloth of his jacket.

When they reached a set of double doors, Ron unlocked them and handed over the keys. "You may as well hang onto them until morning," he said. "There's no one else in tonight."

"No one at all?"

"No, sir. You have the college all to yourself."

"Goodnight then, Ron."

"Goodnight, sir."

The Prof stood for a moment, watching the porter make his way back to Front Quad, the lights along the cloisters looming above him like hazy moons. Locking the outside door, the Prof ascended the stairs to the long gallery, glancing down into the dark void of the dining room where he could just make out the ranks of empty refectory tables glowing pale in the gloom.

He turned the corner into a large room stuffed with comfortable but shabby sofas, an enormous wooden table at one end covered in periodicals. A swift search of the drink's cupboard revealed a bottle of his favourite single malt. Pouring a generous measure, he flicked on a reading lamp and settled down in a deep armchair. He lifted the whisky to his lips, enjoying the medicinal aroma of smoke as it filled his nostrils, the shudder of pleasure as his throat and chest warmed.

Putting down his glass, he took out the box and leaned towards the lamp to study it. He'd been attracted to the crude charm of the chip and notch carvings, but now that he studied it more closely, he found them somewhat disturbing. The patterns seemed to form eyes, then lips, a row of teeth perhaps, or the contours of a snarl. He turned it upside down and heard something rattle inside. Intrigued he tried to lift the lid, but it wouldn't budge. A determination to get the damned thing open gripped him. He worked his thumbs beneath the rim, forcing his fingernail into the groove.

His thumbnail snapped.

Cursing, he nibbled the ragged nail, getting to his feet and retrieving a bartender's knife from the drink's cabinet. He twisted it between the joint. The box gave a complaining squeak. He worked more feverishly, twisting and moving along the groove, his lips pursed in concentration.

The knife slipped, scratching the age-blackened wood and catching the soft flesh of his palm. In a fury, he flung the box down, sucking at the skin between thumb and forefinger. The box sprang open. Something skittering across the floor and into the shadows.

Overwhelmed with chagrin, he lifted the box, inspecting it for damage, wetting a forefinger and dirtying the pale scratch. A strange scent rose from the interior. At first it seemed to hold a vanilla gasp of cedarwood, but as he bent closer, it altered to something primitive and disturbing, like the sickly smell of death. With a shudder he laid the box on the table and searched the floor for the thing he'd seen drop. Pressed up against the skirting board he found a knotted and crudely decorated braid of leather.

Relief overwhelmed him. He'd put it back in the box before delivering it and no one would be any the wiser. He returned to his seat and, with the braid hanging from his palm, he took another mouthful of whisky.

He wondered if the braid could be a prayer rope. It was knotted at intervals, each knot encircling some sort of material he couldn't identify – feathers perhaps, or hair? Others enclosed dull yellow beads and sticks that could have been carved from bone. As he peered and turned the knots, a sly draught began to trickle its way across the back of his neck, scraping a shudder down the inside of his spine.

He got to his feet and walked out onto the gallery above

the dining hall. He felt a distinct drop in temperature, almost as if the mist from the Quads had seeped into the dining room below and was rising silently in the darkness to flow across the gallery, twisting itself around his ankles. As his eyes became adapted to the lower levels of light, the shadows around High Table beneath him seemed to clot, coalescing into a figure seated in the Provost's chair.

The Prof shrank back from the balustrade, his palm and forehead drenched in sweat. As the shock ebbed, he came to his senses, returned to his former position and called down, "Hello. Who's down there?"

The shadow rose and slithered into a deeper blackness.

The Prof moved swiftly back to the Senior Common Room, knocked back his whisky, shoving the box and braid deep into his pocket. He thundered off down the stairs and into Back Quad. He could see the figure clearly now, standing silently on the trim turf, looking off to one side as if uninterested in his pursuit. A student, he thought, drunk as a skunk and wearing some sort of ridiculous fancy dress.

"Hey," he called out, stepping on the grass and approaching. The figure – male or female, he couldn't say with certainty – floated away from him as if on the mist itself and he followed, his irritation rising as he quickened his pace. As he rounded the corner into Front Quad, his eyes were momentarily drawn to the warm glow coming from the windows of the lodge. When he looked back into the cloisters, the figure had gone.

He tapped on the lodge window. Ron jumped to his feet, giving a convincing impression of not having been asleep.

"Did a student just go past?" the Prof said.

"Student? No, sir. I told you, no one's in college over the Christmas break."

"Someone was loitering around in Back Quad. They were on the grass."

"They're not allowed on the grass." The Prof gave him an exasperated look. "I'll check the cameras," Ron said wearily.

The Prof stood behind Ron as he double clicked the camera screen that recorded the door to the Senior Common Room. "Play it back to when I went in," the Prof said. The minutes ticked by. Ron shifted uneasily in his chair. Eventually the Prof saw himself come out, his mane of white hair luminous in the distorted light of the cameras. "Show me Back Quad." Up it came, the manicured lawns as pale a zinc and utterly deserted. "What time was this?" the Prof said.

"Four minutes to midnight, sir."

"It can't be. That student was out there by then, I swear it."

"And here you come, sir."

Indeed he did, walking purposefully towards the lawn, gesticulating at the empty Quad like a mad man, his lips moving in silent pantomime.

"I can check Net2, sir. See if anyone has used their card and come in through one of the other doors." The Prof waited although he knew what the answer would be. "Only you, sir. No one else came in or went out."

"Very well. Thank you, Ron," the Prof said, taking his leave.

"A little less of the single malt, eh sir?"

The Prof ignored the dig, but it worried him. Had he drunk more than he remembered? He walked through to Back Quad, his footsteps echoing eerily around the icy cloisters. He felt as sober as a judge. He let himself into his rooms, took out his bottle of the cheap stuff and poured himself a hearty slug. He wanted to make sure he slept.

The final shot of alcohol fumed in his brain and shortly after rolling under the covers, his daytime thoughts began to fragment. Random images flitted past like a magic lantern – the churning water of a millrace; tiny knives pricking at flesh; the creak of a rope; a creature of exquisite darkness pulsing like the booming shadows of the crypt. He thought he had woken but a blackness slipped across his face. It was of such beguiling softness it felt like velvet, but the velvet was dense. It bowed into his nostrils when he tried to breathe; tightened across his mouth as he tried to fill his lungs.

He woke with the gasp of a drowning man. He was on the floor. He was bitterly cold, his head thundered with pain as if every tooth in his jaw was infected, but there, on the side above his ear, a pain stinging and sharp. He pressed his finger to it. It came away damp.

Getting stiffly to his feet, he peered into the mirror above the chest of drawers. He looked ghastly, his skin drawn and pale, his hair standing up as if he really was a mad professor. He turned his head and lifted his hair. A bright red divot the size of a lentil glistened in the morning light as if a lump of hair had been pulled from his head as he slept.

Baffled he went through to the sitting room. The box sat on the table beside his empty tumbler. Surely he'd left it in the pocket of his jacket. He shook it gently, heard a comforting rattle. The braid was within, and he had an appointment to keep.

THE WALK through the crisp morning air did little to revive his spirits, and his hopes of an interesting morning with Dr van der Berg also took a blow. She was a plain woman with buck teeth and watery eyes. She thanked him, studied the box momentarily and opened it with the expert twist of a palm. She peered inside.

"Goodness," she said, drawing out the braid, "This is very old, seventeenth century for sure."

"What is it?" he said innocently to cover up his vandalism of the night before.

"I do believe it's a Shivering Ladder."

"What on earth is that?"

"It's sometimes called a Salem Ladder. If you'd been cursed and could get your hands on the ladder, you could end your own curse by passing it on to someone else."

"How would you pass it on?"

"In the knot, of course. Each holds something of the person or thing to be cursed. If you want your neighbour's chicken to die, it's a feather. If it's your rival, a piece of hair, a tooth perhaps. So all these people or animals…" she ran her finger down the braid, "Are no longer cursed because they're near the top of the braid but the final knot…" Her expression of interested good humour melted away and she became extremely still.

"What is it?" the Prof said.

Slowly she lifted the braid until the end of it hung before his eyes. He peered over the top of his glasses to bring the final knot into focus. It held a tuft of pure white hair, the tiny divot of skin glistening wetly in the daylight.

First place in category

THE BUTCHER'S BOY'S BICYCLE

Genre: Action/Adventure • **Subject:** A rite of passage • **Character:** An apprentice

Sixteen-year old Patsy and her family may be struggling with wartime rationing but she has no intention of giving the butcher's boy what he wants just to fill the family larder. He's an absolute shocker and besides, Patsy has a better plan.

I found out about the facts of life when I was sixteen years old. My big sister came back from her first week of war work and told me all about it. I was horrified. If I'd sat down and tried to imagine the most disgusting things two people could do to each other's bodies, I could not have come up with that.

"You're pulling my leg," I said.

"Honest truth, Patsy," Jill said. "After the first couple of times, it's the most marvellous feeling in all the world."

"Who told you that?"

She raised a savagely plucked eyebrow and crossed her lips with her finger. That's why, when a few weeks later the butcher's boy gave me a smouldering look over the counter and said, "Do you want to see my meat?" I knew exactly what he meant, and I gave him my very best old-fashioned look.

Stanley wasn't a boy at all. He was plenty old enough to fight but he'd wangled an apprenticeship with Mr Wakefield the butcher pretty much the day war was declared to make sure he was in a reserved occupation. He was what my mother called a nasty piece of work, but he was hard to ignore because he was the only person in that shop to bend the rules. He had a nice little business selling meat on the black market. He would have been in hot water if Mr Wakefield had found out.

Mr Wakefield was in the Home Guard. He was an upright, law-abiding man. He wouldn't dream of slipping a couple of extra kidneys under the greaseproof paper when he was wrapping your meat.

Jill said the family need never want for meat if only I'd be nice to Stanley. But Stanley was an absolute shocker. He was tall and skinny, and his eyes were rimmed in red as if they'd been sewn into his skin with scarlet cotton. His Adam's apple stuck out further than his nose and had a tuft of whiskers sprouting out of it that waved like the antennae of a woodlouse when the lump moved up and down inside his throat. So, all in all, Stanley the butcher's boy was the very last person I ever expected to open my eyes to the future pleasures of sex.

Luckily, I didn't have to follow my sister's advice and make glad-eyes at Stanley. Despite being a girl, I spent my childhood learning how to poach with my big brother

Tommy. What with Tommy out in North Africa fighting Herr Hitler and Jill in the ATS, poaching was just about all a sixteen-year old girl could do for the war effort.

I'd been supplying the family pretty well by setting snares around the hill above the village but recently I'd been coming home without a single rabbit. Someone was getting there before me. I decided it was time to knit myself a long net.

I tied the support cord across the sitting room and worked at the knots each evening, the net growing a few feet every day.

"You need two people to set a net," my father said as I worked behind him.

"Are you volunteering?"

"Not on your nelly. If there's one thing the last war taught me, it was never volunteer."

For the next few weeks, I was up before my parents woke and onto the hill before the sun rose. By watching the rabbits, I worked out their favourite places for sitting and eating. When the buzzards came over, I noted which way the rabbits ran. Then I'd brush the grass off my school uniform and walk back down the steep path into the village in time for assembly.

When autumn came and the moon shrank to little more than a sliver of silver in the sky, thin enough to cut, I waited for the wind to change. Eventually the perfect weather arrived; a mild September evening, the sky black with scudding clouds and the wind blowing from the south. Tonight was the night.

I dressed in dark clothes and pulled on my winter balaclava. It itched like billy-o because Mum knitted it out of old boiled wool, but I had to be careful. The local bobbies would be out, making sure curfew was observed.

It was pitch black as I crept through the village. I'm not afraid of the dark; if I can't see, no one can see me. By the time I started walking up the chalk track to the hill, my eyes were dark-adapted, and I could see the lines of the trees and hedgerows against the paler fields. I reached the foot of the hill and climbed quietly between the strands of barbed wire and into the meadow, working along the hedge and pegging out my net as I went. The wind eddied around me and an owl hooted up in the copse. That was a good sign. They only hoot when all is well.

I'd finished setting the net and was walking the long way round to the top of the field to get behind the rabbits when the clatter of wings and the cackle of an alarmed pheasant made me drop to the ground. Pheasants are the laziest birds in the world. They hate taking to the wing, particularly at night. A fox may have disturbed it, but I had a feeling that something else was out there in the dark, and I felt the skin on my scalp pimpling as if my hair was trying to stand up on end like a cat. Night noises were all around me – the sigh of the wind in the trees, the rustle of a small creature moving through the dead stems of grass, the chatter of a bat as it swooped past me. I rose cautiously to my feet and froze as a stick cracked close by, followed by the rhythmic sound of breathing. I turned slowly and stared at the great bulk towering over me. There was a wet snuffling sound, and I caught the smell of chewed grass. It was a cow.

"Shoo," I hissed and saw the liquid glint of her eye. I pulled one of the netting stakes out of my basket and shoved the cow on her shoulder. She veered away but the great head swung back towards me. I smacked down hard where I thought her nose might be and with a snort she was off, the wet thud of her hooves disappearing into the darkness.

I took a deep breath to steady myself. Tommy had always taught me to take a long route back behind the rabbits and I was well downwind of them. I could only hope that the ruckus hadn't sent them scurrying back into the copse. I moved stealthily up the hill and round behind their feeding area, resisting the urge to peer over the ridge to see if I could spot their dark little bodies against the grass. Nothing was surer to make them scatter in different directions than a human head looming above the horizon.

Eventually I was in position and stood up to start the long and patient walk back towards the net. Tommy taught me to do this with a torch, but it was too risky. The farmer's house sat at the bottom of the track and it was all too easy to spot a light out in the darkness with the blackout. Instead, I tapped a stick against the top of my Wellington boot as I walked, making a clicking sound with my tongue. Below me I could see the occasional swerve of a black blob against the pale grass but mostly I was flying blind, trusting that everything Tommy had taught me would fill the net at the foot of the hill.

I could tell from the steepness of the ground that I was nearing the hedge and I felt a tickle of excitement underneath my ribcage. How many had I caught? Just then I heard a distant and strangled cry, not unlike a newborn baby. It could have been a rabbit scream, but it didn't sound quite right. It was too deep, as if someone was imitating the cry to make the rabbits run. I stopped and strained my ears into the darkness, trying to pick up any unusual sounds above the wind – and there it was, the steady tramp of feet. Could it be my cow again? No. This was human.

I hunkered down behind a tussock of grass. I was close enough to the net to see it twitching with rabbits but there was a dark shadow off to the right, moving slowly towards me. For one awful moment I thought it was the farmer but then the figure crouched down, raised an arm, brought it down swiftly and tossed something over a shoulder. Someone was bagging my rabbits.

Such a fury built inside my chest that I almost launched

myself down the slope and onto the crouching figure but I knew it was madness. There was nothing else for it – I had to crawl away from the hedge and lie in wait, hoping against hope that once he'd picked up all my rabbits, I could go back and retrieve my net.

Moving snake-like up the meadow, I settled down in a fold of land and watched. I counted the number of times the hand came down – it must have been twenty. When I thought of all the sugar and butter and eggs we could have swapped for those rabbits I nearly wept.

The moon sailed high above me in the gaps between the clouds. I could see the figure more clearly now. He was tall and lanky. He made his way down to the track and climbed through the fence. When he kicked aside a pile of straw and hauled a heavy black metal bike upright, I knew it was Stanley the butcher's boy. Leaning the bike against the fence he started paunching and skinning the rabbits before loading them into the basket on the front. He knew what he was doing, expertly flicking the guts away for the foxes to clean up before morning then peeling the rabbits free of their pelts.

Here was my chance. Even if he spotted me, it would take him several minutes to run back up the meadow, time enough for me to flee but if I snatched the net off the poles, there was just a chance I could retrieve it and make my getaway.

I scurried down from my hiding place and started to gather up the net. It snagged on thorns and tangled around the poles. Every now and again I glanced behind to make sure Stanley was still slashing and flicking. I was almost done bundling the net up into my arms when I saw him stop and wipe his hands down his clothes. He'd finished. Only a few feet of net left to gather. I heard a shout and turning, I saw him pushing his way between the wires back into the meadow. I tugged the final pole out of the ground, desperately trying to get the net into a manageable lump. Stanley lumbered up the hill towards me and I ran.

Over the tussocks I swerved, desperate to get into the darkness of the copse at the top of the hill. I could hear his heavy footfall and laboured breathing; he was gaining on me. The net made it difficult to run and I was on the point of flinging it aside and sprinting away when my foot caught in a trailing edge and down I went. I tried to get up, but I was tangled and as I struggled to get free, I heard a voice say, "Hello, little bunny."

Stanley the butcher's boy stood over me. Slowly, he crouched down. I flinched away from his hand. It stank of rabbit guts.

"Don't be afraid little bunny," he said. I pushed away from him, digging my heels into the ground, my fingers working to free my foot from the netting. He crawled after me on all fours, his eyes black as plums, his lips glistening. "We'll have you skinned and opened up in a jiffy."

He made a lunge towards me and I leapt to my feet, grabbing hold of the edge of the net and flinging it across his back. Down I went again but now he was tangled too. I tugged my foot free, scrambled to my feet and plummeted down the hill towards the track. When I reached the fence, I turned and saw him silhouetted against the sky, struggling to get free of the net, his arms waving around his head as if he were fighting off a swarm of bees.

I grabbed that bike of his and set off down the track. It was hard to steer; the weight of the rabbits in the front basket kept pulling me off course. When I dared look back, Stanley had freed himself and was pounding down the track towards me, yelling like a madman. I pushed the pedals with all my might and, as the bike began to accelerate, his shouts faded behind me.

I pushed the balaclava off my head and let the wind blow

through my hair. Faster and faster I went. About halfway down the hill the bike hit loose gravel and began to judder beneath me. I don't know whether it was the excitement of my escape or the surface of the track, but I began to feel an extraordinary sensation. I may not have known exactly what it was, but I was certain I didn't want it to stop.

The bike went faster and faster. I rested my feet on the singing pedals and gasped at the rising sensation in the base of my abdomen. Ahead I saw a light come on in the farmhouse, but I had to keep going, to let the feeling build and as the bicycle hit the hardened ruts of the track at the bottom, a huge feeling of release swept up my lower body. I rattled through the farmyard, a loud wail pouring from my mouth until the bike ran into the barley field at the far end of the yard and I tottered and fell full-length into the crop.

Exhausted with ecstasy, I dragged myself through the barley, far away from the bike. As I lay hidden, my body washed with peace and pleasure, I heard the distant voice of the farmer bellow, "Stop, or I'll shoot."

The slap of Stanley's feet came to an abrupt halt and angry voices drifted on the wind. Lazily I raised my head and peered above the crop. The farmer was poking Stanley towards the bike with the end of his twelve bore, pointing at the bloody evidence of his crime, strewn across the ground. With a sigh I lay back and gazed up at the stars.

Fourth place in category

SPIRIT OF THE NORTH

Genre: Political Satire • **Theme:** Contractual obligation • **Character:** A do-gooder

An idealistic young actor travels to the deprived North of England to direct a community theatre production, but the challenges are not the ones he expects.

A tinny rendition of the *Halleluiah* chorus propelled Jasper across his narrow London bedsit to where his mobile flashed and vibrated, turning gently like a fly on a windowsill.

"Jasper!" Sarah trilled enthusiastically. "Feeling well rested?" His agent's wit was uncomfortably close to bitchiness. Jasper ignored it.

"Have you found something for me?"

"Yes and no."

"What's the 'no' part?"

"It's not an acting role, but I think it's something you're going to like, something you've never done before. A bit of a challenge..."

It would certainly be a challenge if it was a corporate job. Jasper had no intention of pretending to be a Time Lord for MacDonald's fat cats, or organising a whodunnit weekend for a group of IBM execs.

"What is it?" he said tensely.

"Directing."

"Oh! Wow! Yes." He paused. "But I've never directed before."

"Now's the time to start, add another arrow to your quiver. Directors have been telling you what to do for five years now. You've worked with a couple of greats and plenty who couldn't block a drain, let alone a theatre production. How hard can it be?"

"I wouldn't want to let anyone down."

"You wouldn't. You'd be helping, doing some good. Besides, this is an amateur theatre group."

Another bat squeak of anxiety. "I'm not getting paid?"

"You'll get paid – a pretty good fee for theatre. The Coltenham Players have got a grant to stage a community production, part of the government's Levelling Up scheme to regenerate deprived areas in the North of England. Six weekends' work, board, lodging and travel expenses. It's the perfect fit for someone young and eager like you."

AS THE TRAIN MOVED NORTH, the gentrified pastures of the home counties warped into the ugly landscape of disused cooling towers and rusting pitheads. Jasper gazed out of the sooty window at the back-to-back housing along the railway line and, despite his earlier doubts, he felt a wave of excitement. These houses were familiar. He'd grown up in something similar before a council bursary offered him the chance to exchange the boredom of an East End adolescence for the more intellectual boredom of a resting actor. He could do the same for the people who lived up here, those who eked out a living in the shadow of the dark, satanic mills.

The past few months Jasper's inbox had been inundated with emails from Marcus, Chair of the Trustees of the Coltenham Players about the choice of play. Jasper had submitted a preliminary list of suggestions with an appropriate social message – *Hard Times, The Accrington Pals, The Ragged Trousered Philanthropists* – all of which, he was assured, were given careful consideration before rejection on grounds that something lighter would suit the outdoor theatre better. It needed to be entertaining after all.

Jasper was beginning to suspect that his vision of a community who cared deeply about grass roots action may have been misplaced, when the choice of play came through, leaving him baffled but faintly hopeful.

It was Bertolt Brecht's anti-war play *Mother Courage and her Children.*

NIGHT HAD FALLEN by the time his train arrived. It was several degrees colder than foggy London, the smell of a malting factory mixing with a tang of soot. As he exited the station, an elderly man climbed out of a beaten up Volkswagen and hailed him. "Jasper, I assume," he said, clasping his hand and pumping it up and down. "Marvellous to meet you. I'm Marcus." He had a pleasant northern burr. "I'm your host for our casting weekend. Good journey?"

"Long."

"Infrastructure's hopeless up here. The whole railway system north of Birmingham needs overhauling."

As they drove, the streetlights became sporadic, illuminating row after row of run-down houses, shuttered doors, windows staring blindly through cataracts of bent steel security sheets. The derelict streets gave way to darkened roads, flashes of glittering lights at rabbit level observing their progress, the occasional oncoming vehicle sketching the rise and dips of the road ahead. Just once the car bucked, but Marcus's eyes never left the road. Jasper imagined the trail of fur and smashed bone mashed into the tarmac behind, and felt his stomach contract.

"Not long now," Marcus said, turning off the main road. The car bounced along, tossing Jasper back and forth in his seat. As he clutched at the grab handle in the roof, the headlamps caught a sign – Coltenham.

"This is us," Marcus said proudly.

Jasper peered at ribbons of silhouetted houses crouched along a lane as rutted as a farmyard and thought, "These poor people can't even afford streetlamps."

The night was starless, thick black cloud blanketing the sky. When they stopped in a driveway, Jasper couldn't work out where he was in relationship to the rest of the village. A cold blue light shone from a downstairs window across the muddy gravel and Marcus, trudging ahead as Jasper battled to release his rucksack from the footwell, opened the door on a hallway stuffed with rubber boots and overcoats, muddied and torn.

The kitchen was equally run down. Gaps in the frayed rush matting revealed pitted stone flags, a bloom of dirt along the skirting boards, a tidemark on the walls a few feet higher from years of muddy dogs' tails. Despite the unforgiving brightness of the strip light, the room felt cozy thanks to the ancient grease-encrusted range at which stood Marcus's wife Emma, a perpetually grinning countrywoman with English teeth.

"Do sit down," she said, swinging a heavy pan away from the stove and onto the scrubbed pine table. The stew was rabbit. Jasper should have said he was vegetarian.

"I'M INTRIGUED," Jasper said after dinner, postponing taking a sip from the tiny cut-glass schooner that Marcus had filled with something from an unlabelled wine bottle. "*Mother Courage* is a big play. What Brecht is saying about war is slippery and could be interpreted as a representation of class struggle. Is that why the trustees chose it?"

"No," Marcus said with a chuckle. "It's called *Mother Courage and Her Children*. We needed a play with lots of parts for children."

Jasper was confused. "But Mother Courage only has three children and they're fully grown..."

"Yes, yes," Marcus said, patting Jasper on the wrist. "But the thing about our productions is you can have as many people as you want. It's not like real theatre. There's no budget restrictions on the actors, no one's being paid – apart from you. If you want ten children to run on and run off, you can have them."

"But the play doesn't have them."

"Look, we've had lots of different directors, all home grown. Thanks to this generous government grant, we can afford a professional director for the first time. We're excited about what you'll bring to the Coltenham Players, but expectations must be fulfilled. Part of your contract is to include everyone in the community, otherwise it isn't community theatre, is it?"

. . .

THE FOLLOWING morning Marcus showed Jasper the outdoor theatre which was, to Jasper's surprise, at the bottom of Marcus's enormous garden. "So who owns this orchard?" Jasper asked, gazing up the embankment at the amphitheatre carved into the turf.

Marcus frowned momentarily and said, "I do, obviously. My parents – both long gone, bless their souls – were keen am-drammers. The gardeners carved out the terracing in the fifties, and my parents put on little plays, asked their friends. It grew from that. Shall we go in now and kick off the auditions?"

As they walked back Jasper saw the house as it really was – large and detached, walled off from its neighbours and anchored to the land by centuries of history. These people weren't deprived. Their carpets weren't worn and stained because they couldn't afford to replace them – this was miserliness masquerading as tradition, old money in all its scruffy glory.

"As a matter of interest," Jasper began, "why did you apply for government funding for this production?"

A patronising understanding flickered across Marcus's expression. "I see," he said with irritating perception, "You think we should foot the bill ourselves? But isn't that the whole point? There are people in the community who care deeply about the place – the plumbers, the chap who mows our lawns, the cleaners – and there are people like us who have the resources to actually change things."

AUDITIONS WERE A NIGHTMARE. Marcus had clearly not only cast the play himself, but his decisions were common knowledge. Emma had been promised Mother Courage. "Eyes and teeth, my darling," Marcus said encouragingly as she began to read – and she was awful. A woman who would never see fifty again expected to play Kattrin but had no intention of playing her as a mute, ("Worry not," Marcus soothed. "Jasper will pen something in for you."). And as for Eilif, the elder son, it was suggested that if Jasper wanted someone of an appropriate age, one of the young mums could stipple on a beard and pull on the uniform.

"I can't cast it," Jasper said at the end of Saturday afternoon.

"You have to. It's in your contract."

"Where *is* everyone else?"

"What do you mean?"

"I thought this village had a population of a couple of thousand. There must be more young people who'd like to be involved and aren't away at boarding school."

"They wouldn't be interested."

"Who wouldn't be?"

"Those oiks from social housing."

"Have you asked them?"

"Of course not. They're troublemakers. We want to make things as easy for you as possible."

And in a way it *was* easy. Each weekend he travelled up north, was hosted by another bluff villager and spent the days in the orchard trying his best to pull something worth watching out of this troupe of amateurs whose single admirable skill was enthusiasm. By opening night, Brecht had all the creeping naturalism of *The Sound of Music*. It mattered not a jot because the auditorium was packed with smug locals from the gentrified centre of the village, brimming with the confidence of the wealthy. The only thing Jasper was grateful for was that he hadn't told a single London friend that he'd taken the job.

. . .

A WEEK after the run ended, Jasper was back in London, eyeing the thank you bottle of Marcus's sour homemade wine and wondering if he dared take it to the party at the flat downstairs this evening, when Sarah's number flashed up on his mobile.

"How did it go?" she said.

"Don't ask."

"Frankly, I don't care. Fifteen percent of your fat fee is justification enough for me – so well done, Jasper. You must be very proud of yourself. Fancy a walk-on part in *Downton Abbey?*"

"Speaking?

"No."

"I'll take it."

On his way down to the party, the neck of the bottle sticking out from his jacket pocket, he checked his mailbox. He recognised Marcus's backward-sloping handwriting on the manilla envelope and sank to the steps. Inside was a local newsletter. Beneath a smudged photograph of the set and some indistinct cast members, was a review of *Mother Courage and Her Children,* written (naturally) by Marcus.

"This year the Players had a golden opportunity to try something experimental which would appeal to our traditional audiences whilst reaching out to new people and groups. As Chair of the Trustees of the Coltenham Players, I wanted to have a good look at Brecht and see how we could make it feel new, immediate. An odd choice of play, one might think. I cannot agree. It may portray the destruction of the innocent, the virtuous being ruined in a capitalistic world, but over and over again, it's actually about people and, as a Registered Charity we felt it reflected our pride in our community, and our place in it."

Jasper didn't get a mention.

In a smaller box beneath the review he spotted a parish council decision. "The campaign to block street lighting in the village has once again been successful. Reclaim our dark skies!"

Fifth place in category

GERMANY CALLING

Genre: Drama • **Theme**: Mainstream • **Character**: An influencer

A member of the County War Agricultural Executive Committee (War Ag) is horrified to discover his wife has been reported for listening to German propaganda.

England, 1940

Frank Watson drove through sleeping villages and along a stretch of wide river, which glowed the colour of pewter in the darkness. Heavy rain began to fall, sluicing down the windscreen of the old Austin 7, forcing him to drop his speed. He thumped the steering wheel in frustration, a gust of anger sweeping through him. How could she do it to him?

Eventually he came to the town, the noise of the engine

echoing back from the rows of terraced houses. The streets were pitch black and deserted apart from the odd cat that watched him pass, eyes flashing like mirrors in the darkness. He parked in front of the police station, the entrance heavily sandbagged, and sat for a few moments to compose himself, listening to the ticking of the cooling engine. With a sigh, he heaved himself out of the car and walked wearily up the steps.

Pushing his way through the blackout curtains swathed across the doorway, he blinked in the bright light of the entrance hall. It was partitioned off by a reception desk, behind which stood a man in uniform, three sergeants' stripes on his shoulder. He sported a thick moustache and was busy writing in a ledger.

The sergeant looked up with an agreeable smile, but when Frank announced his name and said he had come to collect his wife, he saw the man's eyes harden, like a bicep. Turning away without a word, he opened a cabinet behind him, chose a bunch of keys, and began to unlock a door marked Cells.

"Wait a minute," Frank said angrily, "Mrs Watson has not been arrested."

The sergeant raised an insolent eyebrow. "Nowhere else to put her."

"There are chairs over there," Frank snapped, pointing at a row of ladderbacks along the wall.

The sergeant shrugged. "You coming or not?"

As they descended a dark staircase, the air thickened, heavy with the smell of stale food and urine. Before he could catch himself, Frank felt a pang of anxiety for Joan, humiliated and treated like a common criminal, but he dismissed it – it was nothing more than the habit of a lifetime, thirty years of caring and protecting her. Under any other circumstance he would have challenged the behaviour of the police, but she had betrayed him, and he kept his thoughts to himself.

She sat slumped on the bench at the back of the cell, her face drawn, her hair flattened as if she had just climbed out of bed. She got stiffly to her feet, and without looking at him, slid past, up the stairs and out to the waiting car.

They drove in silence until they left the town behind. When he could stand the oppressive atmosphere no longer, he said, "How could you be so utterly stupid?"

"That poisonous little Land Girl should never have reported me. I was doing nothing wrong. I know lots of people who listen to the English news from Hamburg. If you want to get worked up about this whole sorry event, you should challenge that ghastly constable who brought me in for 'questioning'. He's her cousin, you know."

"Whose?"

"Constable West is that Land Girl's cousin. They were making an example of us."

"Why on earth would they want to do that?"

"To get back at you. We live in a country community. People don't take kindly to your heavy-handed techniques, requisitioning farms that have been in families for generations."

"It's my job. If we don't improve productivity across the whole country, the Germans will starve us into submission – but perhaps that's what you want."

She turned away from him with a sniff and stared out of the side window at the passing countryside.

When they finally turned into the long, tree-lined track up to Manor Farm, he said, "I regret my last remark – it was uncalled for." He was calmer now and needed her attention to explain how serious the situation was. "No one's accusing you of being a German spy, and I'm sure you're not a German sympathiser."

He shot a look at her, but she was still turned away from him. "But those broadcasts are propaganda, pure and simple. The influence that man Lord Haw Haw has on the people of Britain is frightening. His so-called news is a tissue of disgusting lies, designed to frighten the population into believing we're losing the war. He wants us to give up and sign a peace treaty with that sewer Hitler. I can't believe that you, of all people, would want that to happen."

"Of course I don't. I couldn't be prouder of our son, out there, fighting for freedom and democracy. Pip knew what it meant to me to see him following in the footsteps of the brothers I lost in the last war. I'd never want peace with that country. It's just that..." her voice petered out and she shook her head back as if to clear it. The wheels of the Austin 7 crunched on the gravel drive in front of the house, and she said, "Thank goodness we're home."

As he helped her from the car, Frank restrained her by the hand and said, "I must insist, in the strongest possible terms, that I never hear that man's sneering, sarcastic venom in my house ever again. Do you promise me?"

She jerked her hand away and walked up the steps into the house.

A FEW WEEKS LATER, a meeting of the executive committee ended early. Several of his colleagues retired to the local pub, but Frank didn't much care for the watered-down swill they referred to as beer these days. Things were still a bit strained at home, but all the same, he preferred to get back earlier than expected and have a glass of something decent.

Approaching the house, he felt a swell of satisfaction that Manor Farm was such a handsome building, standing at the end of the long drive, bathed in moonlight. It had a pleasing symmetry with three large windows each side of the front door, six on the upper storey and a coat of arms smack in the middle. It looked like a giant doll's house, as if you could swing open the whole of the front and see all the rooms and furniture inside.

As he climbed from the car, he paused. The blackout curtains hadn't been drawn, and the dark windows stared out at him, unlit and soulless. He frowned. Joan had never mentioned she was going out that evening.

He let himself into the front hall, listening for the usual clatter of the dog's claws on the tiles as he rushed out to greet him, but the hallway was dark and still. Surely she wouldn't have taken Buster for a walk this late? He frowned and opened the door into the book-lined sitting room. It smelt of woodsmoke from last night's fire, but the room lay cold and empty in the crisp moonlight. The long case clock ticked gently in one corner, the chubby-faced moon behind the brass dial at the top, gazing down at him with a mournful expression. The clock had rather come into its own with all this blackout nonsense, knowing when to expect a full moon.

A shudder ran through him, pimpling his skin. He moved across to the window like a sleepwalker and stared up at the moon, full and painfully bright in the sky. A bombers' moon.

He had no idea how many of the sorties Pip had flown over Germany. He didn't want to know, didn't want to think of his precious son flying a heavy bomber, deafened by the thunder of the Halifax engines and tossed about by turbulence. He imagined the smell of dirt and oil, sweat and rubber that must fill the hours of boredom as they droned towards their target, hour after hour in the icy dark, thousands of feet above the earth, a featureless blackness beneath them. He imagined the raw agitation thundering in that young chest as the flak rose from beneath and tore away at the fuselage.

With a snort, he stepped back from the windowpane and stared sightlessly at the vanishing bloom of condensation that his breath had left on the glass. Where on earth was Joan? A sly breeze cooled his neck. He turned. The dog was out in the hallway, sniffing the air.

"Buster?" he said.

The dog trotted into the sitting room, his tail wagging from side to side. "Where have you been, old chap?"

Then he heard voices – or to be more accurate, one voice, the tone nasal and superior. He looked out into the hallway. The door into the kitchen at the end of the passage had drifted ajar, a dim light spilling out onto the tiles. He walked stealthily towards it, the dog at his heels, his heart racing like an engine. As he neared the open door, he heard the mocking English tones quite clearly, "...only a person of Mr Churchill's mentality could congratulate anybody, first for shooting unarmed men and secondly on flagrantly violating neutrality..."

Joan was unaware that he'd come into the room. She was sitting on a hard kitchen chair beside a small radiogram, listening intently.

"What on earth do you think you're doing?" he said, his voice low but sufficiently threatening to make the dog slink to the back of the kitchen and sit against the wall, ears flat.

Joan looked up, her face as pale as the moon, her eyes lensed with tears. Frank strode across the kitchen and turned the radio off with a snap, like the breaking of a bone. "The man's a traitor," he said. Joan chaffed at her hairline with trembling fingers. "I thought I made myself perfectly clear. I will not have you listening to that sickening and foul individual."

"I have to, Frank," she said, her voice strained and broken. "I have to know where our son is, what's happening to him. He could be up there now."

"That man broadcasts nothing more than a pack of lies."

"He doesn't. Most of it is wrong, yes – but not all of it.

Sometimes he hits the nail right on the head. It makes you think. The Ministry of Information holds things back, things like casualties and prisoners-of-war. If I listen to what the BBC is saying and then I listen to his account of same news, I might be able work out what's really happening to Pip and his squadron. I must know how many allied bombers have been shot down, and whether any of the crew have been taken prisoner. No one else is going to tell us. It frightens me, the awful things that man says, but I can't not listen, just in case..." and she dropped her head, her shoulders starting to shudder with silent sobs. "I should never have encouraged him," she managed to say. "I should never have let him go."

Her tears were too much for Frank. He drew a chair across and sat beside her, putting an arm around her shoulders. "Come through to the sitting room," he said softly. "I'll light the fire and fix us a drink." He heaved a great sigh. "Or would you rather I sat here while you finished listening?"

"No," she said, and let him lead her away.

FRANK GAZED out of the sitting room window, watching his wife picking daffodils at the edge of the lawn. He was ploughing it up the following day, making space for more vegetables. Still, it was a shame. It had taken years for those daffs to naturalise, but sacrifices had to made.

His position with the War Ag had given him some sway. He'd been in touch with the Ministry of Information and expressed in general terms that his alarm at the insidious influence the sneering broadcasts from Hamburg were having on a number of people he came across during his working day. He put forward the idea that as long as ordinary men and women, who had sons fighting for this country, were starved of official information, they would continue to be influenced by the lies and the propaganda perpetuated by Lord Haw Haw. He'd received an encouraging response – Mass Observation interviews were highlighting the same concerns and consequently, the Ministry of Information was looking into the feasibility of broadcasting official reports of troops and air crew casualties.

Now, when he heard that vile voice down in the kitchen intoning, *"Germany calling, Germany calling..."*, he would take Buster out for a run, and return when he knew it was over. It didn't seem to bring Joan much comfort, but he accepted that she couldn't stop.

His reverie was broken by an abrupt movement from his wife in the distance. She straightened and looked up the drive, the daffodils cradled at one elbow, the other hand tented over her eyes. A bicycle had come into view at the top of the long drive.

She dropped the daffodils, and they spilled like a flash of golden fire across the grass. She broke into a stumbling run as the telegram boy came to a halt. Hanging his head in what looked like shame, he passed across an envelope, turned his bicycle and cycled away as fast as he could.

Paralysed, Frank watched Joan open the envelope. A moment later it fluttered from her hand, and she crumpled to her knees. As he hurried out of the door and down the stone steps, Buster barking at his heels, an indefinable sense of doom filled his body as if an organ deep inside and essential to life was on the point of shutting down. Please dear God, a voice screamed in his head, let him not be dead.

AFTER THE DOCTOR HAD LEFT, Joan slept heavily for the rest of the day. As evening approached, Frank unplugged the radiogram from the kitchen and carried it through to the sitting room. Waiting for the kettle to come to the boil, he read through the wing commander's telegram for the hundredth time.

The aircraft on which your son was the Flight Engineer took off to attack oil installations in Bremen and Hamburg on the 17 May 1940, and nothing further has been heard. You may be aware that in quite a large percentage of cases aircrew reported missing are eventually reported prisoners of war, and I hope that this may give you some comfort in your anxiety.

Just before nine o'clock, he took a cup of tea upstairs and gently woke his wife. As they came down the stairs, Joan leaning of his arm for support, that cool English dammit-get-out-of-my-way voice from Hamburg floated up the stairs.

"Germany calling. Germany calling..."

Third place in category

THE SLOW BURNING FUSE

Genre: Romantic Comedy • **Theme:** A lapse in judgement • **Character:** An ambulance chaser

Max's opportunity to cement his budding romance with Samantha Westbrook is destroyed by the appearance of the dashing Hector Schofield.

A sharp easterly swept down from the Black Mountains, rattling the brightly coloured waterproofs of a couple of tourists as they trudged toward Duntisbourne Hall, a rundown Jacobean pile on the borders of Wales. Max Black, the most recent addition to the guiding team, gazed out across the courtyard, anticipation warming his chest despite the bitter wind.

"You're looking particularly smart today," fellow guide Noel Canterbury said, taking his place at his side. "With those Patrician good looks of yours, even more tourists are going to mistake you for the earl."

Max laughed. “Not today. It’s quiet. I’m not even sure they need two of us on the front door?”

“I go where I’m sent, Max. Best policy in this place.”

It was also one of the reasons Max liked the job. Having retired from his high-octane life in banking, it was relaxing to have no responsibilities. He was free to ponder ways to impress Samantha Westbrook, the new archivist to the Earl of Duntisbourne, appointed at the start of the season. When he first spotted her, her slim build and careful grooming gave the impression of youth, but on closer acquaintance, he made the heartening discovery she was not a great many years younger than himself.

As the two new members of staff, they quickly struck up a friendship. They had a lot in common, both had been divorced for a decade, and both lived alone. They often met up in the visitors’ cafeteria at the end of the working day for a chat and a cup of tea, but Max wasn’t quite confident enough to ask her out.

And there she was now, heading towards them with a small posse of dignitaries. As she neared, she looked directly at Max, giving him a smile of such unbridled pleasure that he felt heat rising up his neck and into his cheeks. Ridiculous. He was behaving like a teenager, not a divorced man of fifty something.

“Good morning, gentlemen,” Samantha said as she came into the hall. “Is it all right if I take this group to the state rooms? They haven’t booked, but I promised I’d show them round.”

“Of course. A few visitors are wandering through on their own, but no one’s on a formal tour.”

As she disappeared, Max felt the power of Noel’s gimlet gaze.

“How are thing progressing with the charming Mrs Westbrook?” he asked.

Max sighed heavily. "It's a slow burning fuse."

"But is it actually lit?"

Before he could reply, a message crackled over the internal radio. "Front door? There's been an incident in the state rooms. One of the visitors has gone over."

"Gone over where?"

"Gone full length over the banqueting table. Caught themselves a nasty blow on the silver centrepiece. An ambulance is on its way. Can someone bring a wheelchair as soon as possible?"

Max had an uncomfortable feeling that Noel was gimleting again. "What?" he said.

"Now's your chance, Max. You're first aid trained, aren't you? And Samantha is out on tour. This is your moment to impress her."

Grabbing a wheelchair, Max hurried towards the state rooms. A small crowd was gathered around an elderly lady, sitting on the floor, her legs splayed in front of her like a rag doll, a quivering hand held to her head. He pushed through saying, "Stand aside. I'm first aid trained."

His heart leaped. Samantha was kneeling beside the victim, but instead of looking up at him with relief, she was gazing into the eyes of a man he'd never seen before. He was dressed in the style someone from the city might imagine people wore in the countryside – jumbo cords, a mustard sports jacket, dark blue shirt, and no tie. The elderly lady rested back on his extended arm as Samantha pressed a man-sized handkerchief to the women's head.

"Max," Samantha said, eventually looking up. "Thank goodness. We need to take her to the front door to meet the ambulance."

Max squatted down next to the elderly lady, resting his hand on Samantha's. He felt a momentary thrill at the intimacy of the gesture before gently lifting the handkerchief. The cut wasn't large, but it was deep. It needed stitching.

"It looks a lot worse that it is," Max said comfortingly to the elderly lady. "Heads tend to bleed a lot."

"I feel such a fool," she quailed.

"No need," Max said. "You should be here in the summer. People go down like ninepins."

As he helped her to her feet and into the wheelchair, he was aware that Samantha was standing very close to the man in the mustard jacket. "I've made bit of a mess of your handkerchief," Max heard her say.

"Don't worry," he replied darkly. "I have another – one for blow and one for show."

As DUSK FELL, Max locked the doors on the last visitors, and made his way across the courtyard to the cafeteria, which stayed open for another hour. Through the lit windows he saw Samantha, seated at their usual table beside the pillar.

He stopped dead. The polished toe of a brogue was just visible around the edge of the pillar. Once through the door, he saw it was attached to the man in the mustard jacket.

"Max," Samantha called, waving him across. "This is Hector Schofield. He helped out in the state rooms this afternoon."

"Still here?" Max said.

A flash of disapproval wrinkled Samantha's forehead and she said, "Hector is catching a train back to London at around six-thirty. I've offered him a lift to the station. It was the least I could do, having made such a mess of his handkerchief." Her laugh, Max thought, was decidedly kittenish. "Sit down, Max. I'll fetch another cup for your tea."

Hector smiled benignly, watching Samantha as she moved across the tearoom. Max watched Hector. He had often noticed that men who retained a thick head of hair past their forties frequently wore it too long. Hector's was brushed straight back from his forehead, curling densely onto the back of his collar. He had the sandy complexion of a redhead, the skin dull and rough across his cheeks, suggesting that as an adolescent he had suffered from acne. Instead of this blighting his good looks it seemed to confirm his manliness, a sign that abundant levels of testosterone had been pumping around his body throughout his adult life. Max took a strong dislike to the man.

Returning with a cup, Samantha poured the tea and handed it to Max. It was tepid.

"Nasty business this afternoon," she said.

"I dropped by the office on my way out," Max said. "They'd rung the hospital. Miss Tingley needed three stitches. She's back home, right as rain."

"A tumble like that can have far-reaching consequence," Hector said. "There's a potential for whiplash injury, not to mention the long-term psychological damage."

"I think you'll find that out here on the borders of Wales, we're made of tougher stuff."

Hector raised an eyebrow and thoughtfully stirred his tea. An uncomfortable silence descended. Samantha attempted to pour herself another cup, but the pot was down to the dregs. She checked her watch.

"Let me get a refill." Hector said.

"Have you time?"

"For you? Always."

Samantha laughed – again. "I'll give you a hand," she said.

Max gritted his teeth, aware that the edge of his nose had lifted, like a snarl. He wiped his hand across his mouth, determined to get himself under control. What on earth was wrong with him? The man was getting on a train to London in an hour. How much of a threat could he be?

They were over by the teaspoons now. Samantha was giggling horribly. She'd lain a hand on the man's arm. He was leaning his great leonine head towards her, no doubt thrilling her with his witty repartee.

Max tore his eyes away and stared at the floor. Should he leave? He didn't want Samantha thinking he'd gone off in a huff, although of course that's exactly what he was doing.

What was that under the table? Something white. He squinted sideways. It looked like a business card. He stretched his leg out and caught the card with his heel, dragging it towards him. Keeping one eye on the jolly couple in the distance, he picked the card up. His lip curled.

Hector Schofield
Solicitor
[Schofield, Lytton & Dangerfield LLP]

Flash bastard, he thought. What chance have I, a tour guide in a run-down stately home on the borders of Wales, compared to a man like that? Then he spotted smaller lettering running along the base of the card. It read:

Personal Injury Law

He turned it over. He frowned. The back was marked with brown stains, one of them a clear fingerprint. He peered. It was blood, dried blood – and running over the top of the stains, the shaky hand of an elderly woman.

Nerys Tingley, 1 Dove Court, Presteigne LD8 2DE
01544 265220

A smile began to relax his face. By the time Hector and Samantha returned to the table, he was positively beaming.

"I think you dropped this, old boy," Max said, holding out the card.

Hector flared his nostrils and tipped his head back, placing the fresh pot of tea down on the table. Something in Max's tone must have intrigued Samantha, because she turned to stare at Hector as he reached out to pluck the card from Max's fingers. Before he could, Max whipped it out of reach and said, "Now who would get a shaky and bleeding old woman to write her name and address on the back of a card?"

Hector didn't reply. Samantha said, "What on earth are you talking about, Max?"

"It appears that your new best friend here is not all he seems."

Hector gave a nonchalant shrug and replied, "I'm a solicitor."

"A particular type of solicitor."

"We handle all sorts – family law, conveyancing. The usual meat and drink of the profession."

"And personal injury claims."

"Occasionally."

Max passed the card across to Samantha, who studied it, her expression darkening. "I didn't see her giving you her name and address," she said. "When on earth did she write this?"

Hector shifted to the other foot. Max noticed with satisfaction that a couple of beads of sweat had appeared on his forehead. "I happened to be outside when they loaded her into the ambulance. I thought she'd appreciate a contact, someone on her side, that sort of thing."

"Is that how you usually go about getting your business?"

Hector had the good grace to look down at the floor, shaking his head, but after a few moments he turned to

Samantha, an ironic smile on his face, and said, "I suppose that lift's out of the question now?"

Samantha didn't deign to reply. Hector took his phone out of his pocket, tapped the screen, held the phone up in the air, and frowned at the screen again.

"No Uber out here, chum," Max said. "You'll have to walk into the village and try the taxi rank."

"You're joking."

"As I said, we're made of tough stuff on the borders of Wales."

MAX AND SAMANTHA watched the dejected figure of Hector Schofield leave the pools of light spilling from the windows of the cafeteria and disappear into the darkness.

"I completely misjudged that man," Samantha said.

"I disliked him on sight. It saved a lot of time."

"And you were right. He was nothing more than an ambulance chaser."

"That wasn't the only thing he was chasing," Max said. "Shall we have that second cup of tea?"

"For pity's sake, Max. Take me out for a drink, can't you?"

"A drink? I'm not sure I can do that…" He watched a cloud of embarrassment wash across her face. He could tease her no longer. "If we're going out on a date, let's at least have dinner."

UNPLACED IN CATEGORY

CARELESS TALK

Genre: Spy • **Theme:** An award ceremony • **Character:** A welder

When a war worker goes to Buckingham Palace to receive her medal for gallantry, she is plagued by guilt.

At eleven o'clock on the dot, Cherry Wardle stood in line, waiting to enter the ballroom of Buckingham Palace. The queue was long. In this, the fourth year of the war, an unprecedented number of people were being honoured, all of them more deserving than she.

The smell of hastily stubbed cigarettes, Brylcreem and mothballs filled the air. The cheerful chatter of the anteroom had ceased, everyone awed by the red of the carpets, dazzled by the gold leaf of the ceilings and the glitter of the chandeliers. Cherry glanced down at the loop pinned to her lapel. Soon the King would hang her George Medal there, in recognition of her bravery. It wasn't bravery that compelled her to act the way she did – it was guilt.

She was very young and naïve when it began. She had gone down to the corner shop in Salisbury where the girls from the bus depot went to buy their cigarettes. She was aware of a handsome soldier choosing a newspaper at the counter. He looked up and caught her eye, and her life changed. His gaze paused on her for a few seconds longer than was seemly, and in that moment, she recognized her attractiveness to men. This new-found power sent a thrill straight down her middle, forcing her to look away as the heat rose in her face.

When she came out of the shop, he was lingering in the sunshine, taking more time than was necessary to light a cigarette. He smiled, flicking the match into the gutter.

"Beautiful day," he said, falling into step beside her.

She nodded mutely, her heart accelerating in her chest. He wore khaki, and the insignia on his sleeve was Polish, but his dark hair was longer than the other service boys. His voice was deep and exotic, his English careful, and his smile – even now the thought of it pinched at her diaphragm. By the time they reached the crossroads and went their separate ways, she knew his name was Stefan Nowak, that he was with the gun battery out in the park, and that they would meet again that evening in the pub in Assembly Street.

Cherry had been out with boys before, most of them mute with shyness. If they were chatty, they only talked about themselves. Stefan wasn't interested in himself – he was only interested in Cherry. He wanted to know everything about her, where she grew up, where her brothers were fighting, what her favourite books were, her favourite food.

In the heat of August, they lay together, hidden in fields of flax. He found the tiny scars on her forearms, and traced the larger one on her chest with his finger. That was where a particularly hot spark had flown inside her boiler suit. He frowned and smiled down at it, intrigued. How on earth did she get a little burn like that?

The Germans had destroyed the Spitfire factory down in Southampton at the beginning of the war, but production had barely paused. All over England, shadow factories sprung up in sheds, workshops and garages. Even a local hotel was used to manufacture parts. They were safe here in Salisbury. The Germans wouldn't bomb it because they used the spire of the cathedral as a marker en route from the coast up to the midlands. As they flew overhead to drop their bombs on Coventry and Birmingham, Cherry and the other all-girl welding teams churned out Spitfires in their thousands. She was incredibly proud of what she did, but she could not boast about it to anyone. She had signed the Official Secrets Act. Even her scars were secret. Instead, she took his face in her hands and pressed her opening mouth to his.

When autumn came, it was unseasonably cold. Raw winds swept down from Salisbury Plains, tiny particles of snow, sharp as pepper on the skin, shivered bare flesh. They could no longer lie in the fields or make love under the stars, but their need for each other burned with a fury. Where could they go to be alone together? Cherry lived with her parents. Stefan's landlady was apparently more terrifying than Hitler. They had to find somewhere to continue their voyage of erotic discovery.

It wasn't planned. It happened quite spontaneously. Cherry had told Stefan she couldn't meet him that evening because she was on lock-up duty at the depot, the last girl out, responsible for dousing all the lights and checking all the doors. But he couldn't bear not to see her. When she stepped out of the side door and into the alley, he came from nowhere. His arms were around her before she'd even turned the key in the lock. He opened the door again and she tumbled inside, clutching onto him. They staggered backwards together, their laughter echoing around the vast atrium as they feverishly pulled at one another's clothes, coming to rest eventually on a pile of dustsheets at the very edge of the concourse.

Oh, the glorious feeling of his skin against hers, the heady pungency of his secret scent, mixing with the metallic workshop smells. After sating their urgent needs, they lay together, she resting on his shoulder as they smoked and talked. When she rolled across him to stub out the cigarette, his gaze was no longer on her. He was staring at the black shapes in the shadows of the workshop, and she was overwhelmed by her own stupidity.

She grasped hold of his jaw and turned his face towards hers. "You mustn't breathe a word of this to anyone," she said, an edge of panic in her voice.

He laughed lightly, reaching up and tucking a piece of hair behind her ears. "I am sure people have guessed we have been making love for months," he said with a languorous smile.

It soothed her that he had misunderstood. All the same, she gathered up their clothes and pulled him after her, away from the workshop. "Hey," he called light-heartedly, "I am cold. Come back with my clothes."

"It's warmer to dress in the corridor," she said, almost breathless in her desperation to get him out of the depot.

That night she struggled to sleep. As another worry sprung to mind, she muted it with the certainty that nothing amiss had happened. Those black shapes in the darkness of the workshop only looked like the nose cones of Spitfires to her practiced eye. Stefan probably didn't even guess what they were. If he had, surely he would have asked her. But he had been too interested in making love to her.

She would gauge the situation tomorrow evening, then

decide if she should come clean, and explain the vital importance of not breathing a word of what he'd seen.

But Stefan didn't come the following evening. She waited outside the pub in Assembly Street for a full half hour. Clammy with fear, she stumbled through the blacked-out streets until she came to the park. She could see the gun battery in the distance, silhouetted against the moonlit clouds. She called through the fence to the soldiers who looked up, one of them climbing down from the top of the wheel where he'd been perched.

"I'm looking for Stefan," she said. The gunner shook his head, shrugging up the collar of his greatcoat against the cold. "Stefan Novak," she repeated.

"Ain't got no Polish chaps here, love."

"He said he was with the gun battery in the park."

"That's us all right, but I've never heard of a Stefan Novak. Sure he wasn't a German spy?" and he chuckled, drawing on a cigarette and sending a stream of sparks out on the wind.

Of course she was sure. It never even crossed her mind. Even after visiting his digs in Station Road, and discovering that Mrs Preece was nothing like Hitler. Mrs Preece, a small woman in her sixties, was kind when Cherry began to cry. "I'm sure he'll write," she said.

Cherry was overwhelmed with the gap he had left in her life, as if a limb had been torn from her, leaving her half a person. But his departure was inexplicable. As the weeks passed, she thought about what the gunner had said.

When the air raid sirens began, and she heard the drone of planes approaching the depot, she was certain the gunner was right. She turned off her welding torch, and lifted the visor of her helmet.

Moments later there was a shuddering whine as if an express train was leaving a tunnel. The detonation sucked the air from Cherry's lungs, and she felt herself lifting, moving fast across the concrete floor. The ceiling panels bulged and burst apart. She crashed into the opposite wall, her welding helmet ringing like a gong, chunks of metal and masonry hammering onto the floor around her. Blinking the dust from her eyes, she stared into the clearing smoke. Her hearing was deadened, pierced with a persistent whistling. Slowly the note changed, and the whistling became the screams of the trapped. People were in the rubble, right next to the store of gas cylinders. They could go up any minute.

The workshop had filled with rescuers, off-duty soldiers and office workers. She dropped down her visor, ignoring the yells of the air raid wardens to get back. As men and women worked in the rubble, digging out the survivors, she grabbed the first cylinder, and began to drag it across the floor, and into the open. Then another. And another. One was already hot to the touch. She could feel the heat through her leather gauntlets. Another was vibrating. The contents had begun to decompose. They could explode at any minute. It was madness. Suicide. But what did she care? She wished she were dead.

THE GENTLEMAN USHER to the King touched her in the small of her back. Three paces forward. She turned to face King George VI, dropping a hesitant curtsey before approaching the platform. She didn't think she could raise her eyes, but as the King placed the medal on her lapel, he spoke. She couldn't remember what he said, only that he looked tired and seemed hesitant. Perhaps he'd guessed she didn't deserve it.

Within a month the factory was relocated to a huge pig shed out towards Trowbridge. Cherry could still smell their faecal tang in the air, horribly human. It chimed with the dirt of disgrace that clung to her. She hadn't shown her medal to anyone outside the family. She couldn't stand their admiration.

"Careless talk costs lives."

However many times had she read those words on posters around the town? Whenever she tried to convince herself that the disappearance of Stefan and the air raid were simply coincidental, a gnomish voice in her head whispered, Why does it matter? You broke the Official Secrets Act.

She had a plan for the medal. Eventually the right moment presented itself. She was working on her own at the top of a ladder, shielded from the others by the wing construction of the partially constructed Spitfire. Surreptitiously she slid the medal from the pocket of her boiler suit. It was an attractive thing, the head of the King on one side, St George slaying the dragon on the other. Closing her visor, she took up the welding torch, and watched the silver along the edge of the medal shiver and melt against the bridging spar of the wing. No one would see it there, no one would know except herself.

She wanted someone more deserving to have the medal, a true patriot who would never be foolish enough to betray his country, intentionally or unintentionally. She'd never meet him, but he would take her revenge on the Germans for duping her, for making her believe she was loved, when in reality she was taken for a fool, and the consequences had been deadly.

Honourable mention in category

THE STONE CIRCLE

Genre: Suspense • **Theme:** A seminar • **Character:** A recreationist

A small group of delegates attending an outdoor seminar for recreationists in the Welsh mountains, underestimate the ancient power of nature.

We are the watchers on the moors.
We are the whistling in the dark.
We are the shadows in the mist.
We are the Cerrig Marwolaeth.

NO ONE HAS COME for years. A plague has swept the globe but not up here. High above the gravel strewn beds of the rivers, the land returned to ancient ways. And then the plague abated.

It is March and a bitter wind is sweeping down from the icy ramparts of Pen-y-Fan, shivering the brackish water that collects at our feet. The whine of a vehicle struggling up the tracks towards the summit drowns the song of the skylarks.

We watch them disgorge, one, two, three and another who is the leader. He has a young and athletic build, but he's short. Had he come when the stones were raised, he would have towered over other men, a king who fed on meat, a colossus who bestrode the mountains of Wales.

He walks to the edge of the escarpment, a man of nature, unaware that he's crushing meadow caps and olive earth-tongue beneath his feet. He fills his chest then raises his hands in worship to the afternoon sun. The others stand and watch. Their clothing rattles and cracks in the wind, the colours vulgar against the landscape.

We are the listeners.

"Behold," he shouts, his voice echoing across the mountains, "*Cylch Cerrig,* the mystical circle of stone at the heart of the Brecon Beacons."

He returns to the group, wreathed in smiles.

"How old are they?" the only girl among them asks as she weaves her way between us, rubbing her hand across the rough surfaces, her fingers picking at the lichen that has taken years to establish.

"Bronze age for certain. Probably even older. There used to be ancient writing on the stones, but the weather up here rubbed the writing away. It disappeared in the 1940s."

"Do you know what it said?"

"It said that if a cock crowed at midnight, the stones would walk down to the River Nedd, but they think it's a reference to an older legend that says the stones visit the River Mellte on midsummer morning." She's looking at him, a frown pulling at her forehead which doesn't seem to want to move. "There's power in this landscape Anabel and over the next few nights, we're going to harness that power and carry it back in our souls."

They set up camp. The wind billows the tents before they're tethered to the ground. Tent pegs bend and tempers fray, but the leader flits from tent to tent, churning up the ground, carrying armfuls of boulders to pin down the fabric. The other men wander off to find firewood. There are no trees up here. The evening meal is cooked on a tiny metal frame, the fumes acrid in the air.

When night falls, a curlew cries, a lonely lament rising up from the valleys. "Is that a crow?" someone says.

"Careful. There's a stone behind you."

They all laugh. They drink, the laughter is louder. The leader is talking. He has been on a quest to find happiness and peace, a modern pilgrimage into the wilds, a determination to push himself beyond his physical limits, to win his battle with body image and personal relationships. The others take it in turns to share, a battle of strengths, a desperate bid to prove that each has experienced hardship in an unforgiving world.

Their experiences are not terrible.

During the night, the fog comes. It rises from the valley, spilling across the edge of the escarpment and weaving wraiths of mist around the tents.

We are the watchers.

A man leaves his tent and stumbles away to squat among the heather.

We are the shadows in the mist.

In the morning a tent has gone, and only three remain.

They search. They wonder. Had the tent blown away in the night? Surely not, it was weighed down with stones. Where are the stones? Perhaps the man had enough and walked back down into the valley. They would have heard him. Not in this wind. But the stones, the girl cries, where are the stones? They ignore her because they want to mourn the weakness and failure of the man who's gone back to the comforts of the valley, because for them nothing is too bleak, nothing too uncomfortable, nothing too cold, not even the windswept moorlands on top of the Welsh Mountains.

Darkness returns. The foxes cry in the night. The owls screech and snap their beaks, the grouse drum their wings deep within the heather. The sky changes, covering the moon and boiling down from the north, the wind rises, carrying snow vertically across the landscape, thundering against the tents and whining around the stones.

We are the watchers.

The girl appears. She is afraid. Her eyes flash white and wide, her hair whips around her head. She crouches at the front of a tent, then waits, shuddering in the gale, arms tight around her body, shoulders bunched and high.

A man climbs out, his clothing loose and flapping. He takes her in his arms, brushes the hair from her face. They do not kiss. He is comforting her. He is strong. She can cling to him. Together they stumble away, towards the vehicle, buffeted by the tempest. The door is whipped from his hand. He helps her in. She points towards the leader's tent, but he shakes his head, climbs in beside her and battles to close the door. Silhouetted inside, they blow on their hands and rub at one another's arms.

The snow thickens. Their heads sink to each another's shoulders. Their metal refuge shudders and shifts. The stones beneath the wheels slide. The vehicle tilts then jumps away, haphazard, untethered and the gale plucks their screams away. The storm engulfs the accelerating shadow moments before it silently plunges into the abyss.

It is an hour until the Equinox. The leader leaves his tent

and stumbles around the summit, his boots crunching through the ice crusts. He cannot believe he is alone. He raises an arm across his face to shield it from the storm. The tents rise like demons behind him. He turns and yells, falling to his knees as they rattle past, into the night. He falls forward, face down on the ground and his shoulders heave.

He struggles onto his feet and heads towards the track where the vehicle used to stand. For some time he is utterly still, apart from when a particularly savage gust thumps against his back, forcing him to stagger forward. Eventually he moves, walking into the wind then lurching back the way he came. His head whips round, back and forth, unable to believe what he knows is true. He begins to plunge around, flailing his arms in front of him like a blind man, pawing the screaming air as if he might be able to feel something he cannot see. The wind momentarily abates.

We are the whistling in the dark.

He is alert, cupping his hand around his ear. As the wind rises once more and flings handfuls of stinging snow into his face, he comes towards us, eyes narrowed, cautious but hopeful. His clothing is dark where the melting snow has soaked the fabric. The wind will chill it and suck the heat from the centre of his body.

He trips over one of us, sprawls face down and lies still. We think he has gone. He lifts his head, rolls onto his back and pushes himself into a sitting position, legs splayed out in front.

The tempest rents a hole in the sky and the moon appears, blindingly bright behind thin ribbons of gauzy silk. He sees us now, but not as we were. We no longer encircle the summit, we are here and we surround him.

We are silent.

We are steadfast.

We are ancient.

The skeins of silk across the moon thicken and clot, drawing the billowing clouds across her face. It is the Vernal Equinox. When day comes, it will last the same amount of time as this night, but not for him. This night will be his longest night. He rallied the others with stories of endurance and triumph, but he is failing. He is trying to untie his boots, but his fingers are clumsy and uncoordinated. He tears at his clothing, tossing himself around to be free of it. His body has taken over, ancient pathways deep within him force him to survive, flushing his skin in a desperate bid to warm the freezing tissues in his limbs. It's a good way to die. He's hot, so hot. His jacket has gone, and he strips off his sweater and struggles, grunting, to pull himself free of the rest of his clothes.

And now the burrowing begins, an ancient urge to bury himself, but he cannot dig into the earth. He crawls towards us, his hands reaching out to us and we part to welcome him. He laughs between panting breaths, curls his body into a ball and lays his head down.

We shift to crush him, bit by bit, but lights come, brilliant white in the sky, a freakish wind beating from above, the sound louder than the drum of the grouse's wings. From the valley below blue lights flash and we move silently away from the body and settle down among the grass and snow before the men on foot appear.

We are the watchers on the moors.

We are the whistling in the dark.

We are the shadow in the mist.

We are the Cerrig Marwolaeth.

SOLE SURVIVOR FOUND FOLLOWING TRAGEDY ON BRECON BEACONS

Early this morning Mountain Search and Rescue teams were

stood down following the discovery of the only surviving member of a group of missing delegates from an outdoor seminar that took place on the Brecon Beacons last weekend. The young American, twenty-three-year-old Conrad Haley was the group's facilitator. Describing himself as an experienced recreationist, he admitted that he had underestimated the speed at which the weather could change in the Welsh mountains.

Earlier in the week the first delegate was found on the north face of Pen-y-Fan, *having apparently wandered off during the night. As appalling weather conditions closed in, it is thought that two other delegates tried to reach safety in a Range Rover but experienced difficulties on an unmarked track and plunged to their deaths. The names of the victims have been withheld until the families have been notified.*

This is not the first time that tragedy has struck visitors to the famous Cylch Cerrig, *which in Welsh means* Stone Circle. *Local farmer and volunteer member of the Mountain Search and Rescue team suggested the mystical circle of stones at the heart of the Brecon Beacons should be referred to by its more ancient name,* Cerrig Marwolaeth, Stones of Death.

"Perhaps then people with little or no experience would think twice before heading up there. This tragedy could have been avoided with proper planning and preparation, checks on the weather forecast and some understanding of the skills needed to get out of trouble. The mountains round here don't take kindly to being underestimated."

Fourth place in category

THE BODHRÁN

Genre: Romantic Comedy • **Theme:** Loyalty • **Character:** A rhythmist

A discontented woman finds something in her husband that she had forgotten was there.

Bridie Kelly walked slowly through the evening twilight, filtering down through a canopy of summer leaves. A tendril of nostalgic memory reached out to her across the suburban landscape and for a moment she forgot she was walking the dog through a park in the far-flung outskirts of London. Lifting her eyes to the horizon, she momentarily expected to glimpse the ramparts of the Purple Mountains along the skyline. Instead, she saw row upon row of identical houses built in the 1950s and only affordable if someone in the family was bringing home a six-figure salary.

A car drew up outside one of these identical houses – her

house in fact. And there was the man whose insurance firm brought in the six figures that allowed them to live here, her husband Padraic, returning from the one evening a week when he was out from under her feet. He climbed out of the passenger's side of the car, clutching a lapful of paraphernalia to his body. It baffled her daily that he ran a successful business, or that anyone could tolerate working with him at all. She was frequently amazed that his team put up with his rackety way of doing things. He turned to speak to the driver, crouching over as he shed a book here, a sheaf of papers there, and finally that ruddy oversized tambourine, which hit the pavement with a sonorous boom before tipping over and coming to rest at his feet.

The driver leapt from the car and ran round to help, trailing flowing shawls and ethnic prints. Maeve O'Brien, a woman equally as ridiculous as Padraic, that matted grey hair snaking down her back in thick braids as if she was the singer with Clannad, not the hippy grandmother who ran the folk club in a sordid room above a pub in the high street. "I was a child bride," she would trill merrily whenever someone expressed surprise that she had a granddaughter.

Bridie watched her gather up the fallen items and press them into Padraic's hands as he ineffectively sashayed around her. When she retrieved the tambourine, she brushed a sleeve gently across the skin, looking up into Padraic's face for just a few seconds too long before handing it to him and glancing away with the coy tip of the head. Bridie heard him murmur something and clear his throat, that annoying habit he had whenever he'd said something he imagined was amusing. She felt a flash of irritation, an emotion Padraic frequently produced in her, but something was infinitesimally different, a resentment that was uncomfortably close to jealousy.

Maeve O'Brien returned to the car and drove away, an

arm festooned with bangles and friendship bands waving goodbye through the open car window. As Padraic walked towards the light of the porch, Bridie could clearly see a smile on his face.

She clipped the lead onto the dog and hurried across the road. Padraic was still in the hall, shedding his pile of clutter.

"Shall I take your tambourine?" Bridie said icily.

He gave her a sad smile and replied, "It's not a tambourine, Bridie."

"Saw you getting cosy with the granny."

Padraic remained silent.

"So what did you get up to tonight? A rousing chorus of *Michael Row the Boat Ashore* while you stood at the back rattling your tambourine?"

He gave her that tolerant nod that exasperated her. Why could she never get a rise out of him? She wished he'd pull up his big girl pants just this once and show her he still had a bit of fight left in him.

But perhaps he never had any fight in him. Was that the reason she was drawn to him twenty years ago, sitting at the back of the pub in Kilkenny, discreetly tapping the table with his fingers instead of clattering his steel-tipped shoes on the floor boards, arms at his sides, like the lad who'd broken her heart a dozen times or more? Padraic, with a stable job waiting for him on the mainland, seemed manna from heaven compared to the heights and troughs of that heavy drinking step-dancer from County Sligo.

"Come to the Club next Thursday," Padraic said, ignoring her barbed comments. "Come and see for yourself." There was no sarcasm in his tone, no anger in his voice. He was too dull to even lose his temper.

"I'd rather eat my feet than spend an evening listening to songs about oak trees and diseases and all the terrible things the English have done to Ireland for eight hundred long years," she shot back.

"I think Maeve would have a different interpretation of traditional Irish music."

"Oh, Maeve. Yes, the sexy grandmother. I'm sure she'd have a different interpretation for a whole pig's bladderful of Irish traditions."

"There's nothing wrong with being loyal to your roots."

"And I'm not?"

Padraic smiled softly and slipped away upstairs.

Bridie grappled roughly with the dog, trying to unclasp the lead from its collar. Once freed, the dog slunk away into the living room, adopting a watchful position on the hearthrug as if it was painfully aware that its master had openly criticised his wife.

Loyal to your roots, Bridie fumed as she emptied the dishwasher, crashing the cups and plates into the cupboard. What was there to be loyal to? The miserable childhood, or worse still, the miserable Catholic childhood? Admittedly she missed out on the poverty and the shiftless loquacious alcoholic father, but she'd had plenty of the defeated mother, the pompous priests, and the bullying schoolteachers.

THE FOLLOWING Thursday she waited until Padraic left, nonchalantly flicking through a magazine while EastEnders was on. Once the whine of the grandmother's car disappeared round the corner, she grabbed her hooded walking coat from the cupboard, climbed into her car and drove to the high street.

Pushing her way through Londoners at the bar who seemed to think Thursday was the new Friday, she climbed the staircase at the back of the pub and joined the group of people waiting by a makeshift table to pay their entry fee. She dropped a £5.00 note into the plastic cup and, putting up the hood of her jacket, stepped into the room above the pub.

The first thing that struck her was the smell. Without the fug of cigarette smoke, she was powerfully aware of the aroma of bodies and beer mixed with a medicinal scent wafting from a jar of incense sticks burning on the small bar in the corner. As she reached across to collect her complimentary half pint of Guinness, a new smell, the faintest tang of patchouli oil, caught her by surprise, teasing out tendrils of memory of a time when an evening like this would have been an opportunity to find a mate and make love.

At that moment a murmur of approval gave way to the jaunty sound of a fiddle accompanied at first by an accordion. Unable to see the performers, she assumed no stage had been set up to lift them above the crowd. They would be sitting on chairs or standing at the front of the crowd as they would at any craic in a pub in Kilkenny. Heads began to sway back and forth and, as the people pressed forward, Bridie felt a second stirring in the centre of her body as if an invisible thread was drawing her back down the years.

A penny whistle joined the refrain, and the bodies began to move up and down, feet beginning to tap, but when the drumming began, a great roar of approval went up from the crowd. She could have sworn that she heard a group of young women behind her murmuring, "Padraic," with a swoony reverence, but before she had a moment to interrogate them, the rhythm of the drumming picked up her heartbeat. Waves of excitement flooded her diaphragm, and she pushed further forward, determined to see who played with such dexterity and passion.

When she saw Padraic bent in concentration over his ridiculous tambourine, habitual irritation pressed in. He was a middle-aged man making a fool of himself and she had to stop him, but as she watched his wrist flicking the beater back and forth across the skin of his instrument, knocking at the edge, thundering across the taught body of hide and heard the room erupting again and again with each virtuoso change of tempo, his appearance seemed to alter. The flabbiness around his chest and arms now looked stocky and tightly packed, the hair across his head that she thought was thinning seemed close-dropped, accentuating a pleasing symmetry and balance to his face. Those eyes that had gazed apologetically at her for years, crackled tonight with blue fire. When he turned them towards the whistle player, who was none other than the grandmother, her felted braids tossing like snakes around her head, Bridie thought the green-eyed monster would gobble her all up and not even bother to spit out the gristly bits.

She shoved the hood of her jacket off her head and stared at Padraic with such intensity she was certain he would feel it and look her way, but he went on drumming, went on breathing heavily with emotion, and went on holding the connection with Maeve. Bridie called his name, "Padraic," but it was lost among the other voices chanting the same name. Sweat poured off him, but instead of repelling her, as it always had, she wanted to slide her hand through it, along his neck and down between his shoulder blades. All the time, despite the conflicting emotions rattling through her body, she couldn't stop herself from submitting to the beat of his drum, allowing him to move her back and forth, her body twisting to his rhythm, writhing at his tempo until tears began to course down her face. When the tune reached the end, she was utterly exhausted. Melting back into the crowd, she drove slowly home, her hands gripping the steering wheel so tightly that her knuckles glowed ghostly white.

. . .

BRIDIE SAT in the darkness of the living room. When the headlights of the grandmother's car swept in an arc across the walls, she didn't stir. She heard Padraic clattering into the house, murmuring a welcome to the dog who had slunk out to greet him. His shadow filled the doorway and after a moment of silence, he said, "Would you like a light on?"

"No, thank you," she replied.

He came into the room and, standing in front of her, he sniffed at the air. "You came to the Club?"

"I did. I saw you and Maeve. Your connection is very..." she almost choked on the word, "...passionate."

He shook his head slowly. "Only for the music, that I promise you."

She got slowly to her feet. "It's not a tambourine, is it?"

"No. It's a bodhrán, but I think you've always known that."

"And the little stick?" she said, now running her hand up the forearm that had so expertly manoeuvred it across the skin.

"I think you also know what that's called – the tipper."

"But what sort of a tipper?"

"I prefer a hard tipper." He didn't even clear his throat.

"Would you play, just for me."

"You only have to ask."

"Would you play even if I don't ask?"

"Why would I do that?"

"Sometimes just to shut me up, but mostly to remind me."

"Of home?"

"Of that, and many other things."

SECOND PLACE IN CATEGORY

A DISH SERVED HOT

Genre: Thriller • **Theme:** Exile • **Character:** A philanderer

Revenge may be a dish best served cold but when a heartbroken cellist delivers her coup de gras to a cheating pianist, it's smoking hot.

I slip into the concert hall through an unassuming door in the alleyway. Once inside, I move swiftly. I know my way around. I should. This was my alma mater, my sanctuary, my home, my family ever since leaving music college. Now it is another country. I am an exile.

The reason for my banishment? I'll come to that later. For now, there's a lot to do and only the length of an afternoon's rehearsal to do it.

I move cautiously towards the stairs that lead down to the dressing rooms. I peer over the banister before taking the final steps into the corridor below. You can't be too careful, not when someone's issued a restraining order against you.

The acoustics in this building are odd, the sound of the orchestra clearer in the basement than in some of the seats above. I can hear Dante Connardo flinging handfuls of notes at the keyboard, and the orchestra – my orchestra until a month ago – rising and swelling around him. He'll be building up quite a sweat I expect. Let's hope he hits the cadenza in Prokofiev's Second Piano Concerto with even more ferocity tonight.

I move swiftly along to Dante Connardo's dressing room and let myself in. Pausing for a moment with my back against the door, I catch my breath.

A wave of nostalgic longing overwhelms me, pinching spitefully at my stomach. The room smells exactly the same as it did on the evening that he led me tenderly by the hand and we made love surrounded by the warm scent of dust and the vanilla tang of old wood. I remember the intensity of those snatched moments, the sincerity of his promises in the minutes leading up to a concert.

"I will see you very shortly," Dante said darkly as I left first to take up my position with the cellos. How my heart sang as he strode onto the stage. Straddling my cello, my playing was imbued with a certainty that Dante and I felt the emotion of the music as one.

With a snort I pull myself back to the present. I wish I could understand why, after so much blood under the bridge, I still held tender thoughts about Dante Connardo. Ah, well. Perhaps I'm not bad to the bone after all.

Before hunting out his dress suit, I can't quite resist having a bit of a poke around the room. A couple of tumblers stand on the dressing table in front of the mirror. Beside the glasses sits a half empty bottle of Frascati, beads of condensation clinging to the side. Drinking at lunchtime? Dante used to tease me about that, said it was so English. All the same, he should have put the bottle back in the fridge. Seems a pity to waste it.

I pour a hefty slug into one of the glasses. I raise it to the light and there, clearly visible, is a blur on the glass where he must have laid his lips. I run my tongue slowly across the mark, closing my eyes as I remember the wet warmth of his kisses. My eyes snap open. It tastes of cherry. It's lip gloss. Bastard!

I splash the wine into the second glass and drain it in one. The alcohol hits my empty stomach and fumes in my head. I plonk the glass back down with vigor, resting my hands on the table to compose my fury.

So, he's still servicing that viola player, Candida – I mean, a viola player for pity's sake. Those failed fiddle players are the butt of all our jokes. Whoever heard of so-and-so, the brilliant viola player?

The alcohol is beginning to calm me. I lift the bottle to my lips and drain the rest of the wine in several gulps. I wipe my hand across my mouth and realize something has changed. In my distraction, I've lost concentration, allowed myself to be sidelined.

Cold concrete pours into my guts. The music has stopped. Chairs scrape across the floor just above my head. Then – tap, tap, tap – and, "Twenty minutes everyone. See you back here on the dot of half-past."

I can already hear the patter of feet on the stairs down to the basement. I dart across the room and cram myself into the cupboard just as the door into the dressing room is flung open with a bang.

Unable to stand at full height I press myself further back. As my eyes adapt to the gloom, I realize there aren't many clothes in here at all, certainly not enough to mask me should he choose to open the cupboard door. But I needn't have worried. Less than a minute later, I hear a discreet tap on the dressing room door, Connardo's footsteps across the room and his warm tones saying, "*Amore*, Annabel."

Annabel? Who the hell's Annabel? I wrack my brains and it comes to me – Annabel, trilling away behind the violins, her dead straight hair falling across one eye as she purses her pretty little lips into a perfect embouchure. Good God! He's moved onto the wind section.

They've gone silent now apart from the rustle of clothing, the creak of their weight leaning on the dressing table. Was that the slurp of a kiss? I almost burst out of the cupboard, if only to relieve the appalling crick in my neck. For the love of God, how far can they go in twenty minutes?

Not that far, as luck would have it. The empty bottle of wine must have caught Dante's eye because he says, "*Cavolo*! You finished the wine?"

"No," an insipid voice replies. "It must have been you."

"I am Italian. I don't need wine…" and the heavy breathing starts again. I screw up my face in disgust and press my hands onto my knees to relieve the extreme pain in my back. Twenty minutes has never seemed so long.

Finally, I hear the sound of instruments above squawking and parping. There's a snort and a, "*Dio santo!*" followed by a scrabble of activity and a, "Where's my shoes?" "Here!" "Your blouse is undone." "Your zipper!" and the disgusting pair scuttle off to rejoin the orchestra.

I burst out of the cupboard, stretching my aching back. I wait for a moment, breathing with an open mouth until I hear the orchestra strike up, until I hear the distinctive thunder of Connardo's hands on the keys.

I snatch the dress suit from the rail and slide the dress pants off the hanger. Taking them across to the dressing table, I carefully turn them inside out. You can tell they're expensive. The inner seam is beautifully bound in bias silk to protect the inner thighs of the maestro. Nothing must disrupt the concentration of the great Connardo.

As I execute the next stage of the plan, I remember dining at his flat. As with everything else in his life, he cooked with passion and drama. His specialty was pasta arrabbiata, so hot it made me cough.

"It is good, yes?" he said, looking across the table at me, his eyes as dark as plums.

"It's lethal," I said, fanning my open mouth with a hand.

"Chili is sublime," he said. "It stimulates the endorphins. It makes you happy, yes?" It wasn't the chili that made me happy, it was him.

Not at first, mind you. His reputation had preceded him. I was determined to dislike him. I'm not sure what I expected of this virtuoso of the music world. Devastating good looks? A oily Italian charm? Instead a gangly, self-deprecating man turned up, somewhat disheveled with long hair and olive skin. Nothing like his on-stage persona. He sought my opinions, seemed to value them and before long I was the envy of the string section – his confidante, his lover.

God, I was so naïve. When I found out about the viola player, I was devastated. I tried to reason with him, again and again. He told me not to be *cosi arrabbiata* – so angry. I was more than bloody *arrabbiata* – I was furious. I knocked over a vase of flowers in his dressing room. He said I'd thrown it at him.

He spread horrible gossip about me. Percussion were delighted to embellish. When the string section got wind of it, they passed it on to brass. I became the laughing stock of the orchestra. I thought my humiliation was complete.

Then his complaints began. He claimed someone was out of time – me. Every rehearsal, every performance, he blamed my playing for his loss of concentration. He said I straddled my cello in a provocative way. Said I never took my eyes off him for the whole of the concert. He wanted me moved out of his sight line. His tantrums became so fierce, the musical director took his side, said I was no longer a good fit for the orchestra. In despair I begged Connardo to intervene on my behalf, retract his accusations. He accused me of stalking. I was exiled from the orchestra, banished from the concert hall.

IT'S time for the evening performance and what a performance it promises to be. I wouldn't miss it for the world. I've taken a box, all to myself and spent the afternoon working on my disguise. Nothing too elaborate. That might call attention to myself. Instead, I'm dressed in charity shop beige, hair scraped off my face, bobble hat pulled over my eyes, scarf across my mouth. Good job no one bothers to dress up for provincial concert tours anymore.

I shuffle forward with the rest of the audience, head down, heart fluttering with anticipation as I near the foyer. I'm through the door. All of a sudden, my legs feel boneless with exhaustion, threatening to buckle beneath me. I take a deep breath. I glance across at the box office. They're too busy with collections to look up.

I'm moving up the stairs, insulated by the plodding line of concert buffs. A woman behind me croons excited praise for Connardo. Someone's up ahead, checking tickets. My heart makes an unpleasant movement in my chest.

I risk a glance as I reach the top of the stairs. The usher's new. I don't know her. The anxiety sinks like a drop in pressure in my brain. She tears my ticket and I move past her, desperate now to make the sanctuary of my box.

"Excuse me?" she calls.

I keep moving.

"Madam!"

A hand touches me on the shoulder. I spin round, my face coloring in that feverish, guilty way.

"Your stub, madam – in case you want to visit the bar during the interval."

"Thank you," I say, my voice unbearably tight in my throat.

I fall into the box and press myself into the shadows at the back. The sound of the audience taking their seats is soothing. I slide forward. The hall shimmers red and gold in the semi-darkness like the gilded recess of a vast cavern.

The orchestra comes in. The applause swell for the conductor. The audience rises for Connardo. I smile. He looks handsome in evening wear. He sits at the keyboard as the orchestra begins. He's composed in his arrogance, uninterested unless he's playing. He barely deigns to glance at the conductor before he begins. The look of rapture on his face is so intense it's as if he has a bad smell underneath his nose – rather like his sex face, I think.

My mind begins to detach itself from my surroundings and glide over the sound. His playing is dazzling. His energy increases. I peer down, my heart accelerating with girlish glee. He's hunched over the keyboard, his focus extreme, his breathing heavy. Sweat is beginning to flick off the tips of his long hair. He's struggling, throwing himself around. The cadenza reaches a climax. I can feel anticipation pouring off the audience. His muscular physicality thrills them.

He stops playing abruptly. A gasp goes up from the auditorium. He's on his feet, throwing himself around as if he's still playing the cadenza. His fingers are no longer running up and down the keys. They're plucking at the inner seams of the dress pants. He staggers from the stage, legs bowed as if straddling a cello and disappears from sight. The orchestra plays manfully on, thin and reedy without the piano.

I imagine the scene backstage. Connardo, tearing off his

dress pants. Staring at them, baffled. I wonder if he'll guess. Perhaps he'll think Candida from the string section has given him a dose. Or Annabel from wind. I'm rather hoping that if he's sufficiently *arrabbiato* he'll make the connection. Perhaps when those endorphins kick in. "It makes you happy, yes?"

Chilis, pureed, massaged into the inner seams of the dress pants and dried with a blow dryer. Perfectly innocuous until the inner thighs begin to sweat.

My task is done. As I slip through the empty foyer, I feel a sort of giving way around my heart, a caving in, like the slither of sand through the waist of an hourglass. It's the sickening realization that my exile is now complete. After tonight there will be no reprieve. I've served my revenge piping hot and yet, inside, I'm icy cold.

Fifth place in category

THE TONDEUR OF MARSEILLE

Genre: Horror • **Theme:** A rental • **Character:** A hairdresser

When Julia goes to Marseille for her future sister-in-law's hen party, she stumbles into an ugly carnival of evil from many years ago.

Julia stood in the cobbled street, staring up at the lighted windows of 6, Rue Saint-Nicolas. When Marie said she'd booked a gîte for her hen party, Julia had imagined a cottage out in the country with roaring fires, not a town house in the old part of Marseille in the middle of winter.

She'd been dreading the weekend. Naturally, she was delighted her brother was marrying Marie. She was a lovely girl, but Julia didn't know her very well. She certainly didn't know any of the other girls coming on the hen weekend.

She pulled hard on the doorbell chain. There was a faint chime deep in the building followed by a chatter of distant voices. She gazed along the empty street. A glimpse of water glittered down by the quay. Enameled shop signs creaked gently on their brackets, illuminated by the wall lights, looming out of the darkness like hazy moons. Distractedly, she noticed a blue plaque on the house next door:

George Fourniret
Le Tondeur
26 Août 1945
Assassiné par la Résistance.

A sly shiver bobbled the skin on the back of her neck. She stamped her feet against the cold. The sea mist was oozing from the stones, chilling the air around her ankles.

The door flew open. Her eyes darted around the boiling crowd of cheery friends. She couldn't see Marie. The girls rushed forward, reassured her that Marie was busy. She'd be down soon. They introduced themselves. She instantly forgot their names. They swept her through the vast hall and onto the kitchen.

A girl with a cornrowed braid pressed a drink into her hand while a redhead with lustrous waves hacked away at a French baton, slavering it with soft cheese and insisting she eat something.

"Come on through to the sitting room," a girl with a sleek long bob said.

"Let's get this fire lit," a girl with a side-swept bang said. Cautiously, Julia came to help, rolling balls of newspaper up and chucking them in the grate.

"Is this a good idea?" Julia said. "It doesn't look as if it's been used for ages."

"Let's see," the girl said, putting a match to the paper and piling the kindling sticks on top. They crackled appealingly. A grey plume of smoke headed up the chimney. "There," she said, "It's drawing fine."

"Did you have much trouble getting here?" another girl asked.

"No," Julia said. "I tried my very best schoolgirl French on the taxi driver. He looked at me as if I was speaking Russian…"

"The French all do that."

"Then he started to laugh. He said, '*Le maison de pute?*' I said, I didn't understand, and he said, '*Le maison de prostitution.*'"

"You understood that all right."

"You bet."

"This was a brothel during the war," the blonde said. "There are pictures in the house book, photographs from years ago." She pushed a loose-leaf binder towards Julia and said, "Have a look."

As the girls talked and drank, Julia flipped through sheets of recommended restaurants, city walks and shops until she came to a section marked, History. The pages were illustrated with poorly scanned sepia photos. There was the old port in 1920, filled with traditionally rigged tall ships. She found a picture of the house in the 1930s. A group of women lounged on the steps, smoking and staring insolently at the camera.

The women on the following pages looked very different. Surrounded by jeering crowds, they bent their heads as men hacked at their hair. In another photograph, they were paraded through the streets, barefooted and bruised, clasping their ripped clothing to their breasts. The caption read, "The Liberation of Marseille, 1945".

"Horrid, aren't they?" the girl with the bob said, plonking herself down beside Julia. "Did you see that plaque on the wall outside?" Julia nodded. "He was man who did it – the tondeur. Nothing but a second-rate hair cutter. Turned out he was a petty collaborator himself. Maybe he thought if he scalped the sex workers, no one would think he was a traitor. He was wrong. He was shot by the Resistance."

A crash from above silenced them. "What the hell was that?" the redhead said.

"It's probably a loose shutter," another girl said.

"Or the plumbing," someone else said. "It obviously hasn't been serviced for years. I pulled a rope of black hair out of the plughole in my bathroom."

"Shall I go and see?" Julia said.

"Not on your own," everyone chorused.

"I'll come up with you," the girl with the bob said.

The combination of a long journey, not much to eat and several glasses of wine had made Julia feel light-headed and jumpy. "I'll take my things up," she said. "I think I'm ready for bed." Wearily, she struggled to her feet, pulling her backpack onto her shoulder.

The girls climbed the staircase, the wood creaking under their feet. A breeze curled down towards them. "There must be window open," her companion said. Julia felt a tingle along her scalp as if her hair was trying to stand on end.

"I should tell Marie that I'm here," Julia said.

"She'll be around somewhere."

Julia followed her into one room after another. "Only your room left," the girl said, opening the last door in the passage.

Julia snatched at the girl's forearm. On the opposite side of the room hovered a spectral shape, pulsing like a giant jellyfish in the icy depth.

"It's the curtain, silly," the girl said, striding past and pushing aside the full-length voile. She banged the window shut. "Well," she said, dusting her palms, "I've no idea who left that open. It's freezing in here. Do you want to bunk down with me next door?"

"I'll be fine," Julia said. That wine had really gone to her head. Without undressing she climbed under the covers and went to sleep.

She woke with a start. It was pitch black in the room, barring the pale shapes of the voile, hanging at the windows. The house was silent except for a clicking sound. She pushed herself up against the pillows and tilted her head, listening. Was it the old wood of the building contracting with the cold of the night? Or one of the girls, clicking across the floorboards in a pair of high heels?

She sniffed. There was an odd smell in the air.

She sat bold upright. Something was burning. It smelt like wool. She should have reminded them to make sure the fire was safe before everyone went to bed. In a house as old as this, a fire would spread in minutes.

She climbed out of bed, snatched up her phone and flicked on the torch. She wished the beam were brighter. She could only see the ground at her feet. She stepped out into the corridor. The smell was stronger. It made her eyes smart. She should wake the others.

She rushed next door. "Wake up!" she said, her voice high with anxiety. The beam from her phone trembled as she shone it across the room. It caught the bedding, tumbled from sleep. It reached the pillow.

Her body felt momentarily boneless. The bed was empty.

In panic, she stumbled along the corridor, flinging open door after door. No one. She stumbled down the stairs. At the furthest reach of the torch, the darkness lightened and coagulated, swirling shapes past her.

She put her hand on the door into the sitting room. Her heart bumped unpleasantly in her chest then began to race like an engine with no connection to the rest of her. She opened the door.

There were no flames, nothing but a gleam of ash in the grate. The band of embers bloomed more brightly as she approached, the glow almost comforting, like an autumn bonfire at the end of the garden at dusk. But the smell wasn't comforting – it was sulphurous and rank, the stench of burning hair. Hanks of it were piled up on top of the embers.

As she stared at the sweating pile, inert with confusion and an indefinable disgust, her consciousness was invaded by that distant sound of clicking. Although she didn't fully trust her legs, she forced herself back towards the hall.

Other sounds reached her – cries of dissent, the crash and scrape of a piece of furniture followed by a moan of fear. She headed towards the sound. The floor beneath her feet was strangely slippery, blotched with black swirls. She reached down. Her fingertips touched something silky. She drew it up into the light of her torch. It was a curl of hair.

A muffled scream came from the end of the corridor, tailing off to a high-pitched whimpering, as sickening as the cry of a fox in the dark. Cold night air flowed towards her, shivering her skin. Ahead she could see a patch of pale grey. A door to the outside courtyard was open.

She stumbled on, her heart fluttering in her throat, her ears filled with that terrible sound of clicking as if the dead had risen from the catacombs below and were pursuing her with chattering teeth. The weak beam of the torch skittered over the walls. Writing. Graffiti. Ugly and hurried, bright red as if scratched in blood.

Collaboration horizontale!

Putain!

Traitre!

The air inside the courtyard was clamped with cold, the surrounding buildings so high the weak light of the night sky hardly penetrated its depths. Wraiths of mist moved stealthily around the walls, curling against shapes she couldn't quite make out.

She took a step forward. The shapes began to merge into recognizable forms. She felt her heart pinching, caving in, collapsing before fluttering weakly, inefficiently.

She couldn't tell the girls apart. Could that be the redhead? Or there, the girl who had the braids? They were all stripped to their underwear, their hands and feet filthy and lashed to chairs. The bruises of savage blows and kicks covered their exposed flesh. Their shorn heads glowed ghostly white, dappled with tufts of hair that had escaped the vicious shearing. Their scalps were latticed with cuts, the blood black against their shoulders in the monochrome hell of the courtyard.

"Help us," one of the girls said, her eyes as wild as a hunted animal.

The clicking began again. It was right behind Julia. The blood drained from her body. She turned. The razor-sharp blades of the shears flashed, the malevolent glee on the face of the shearer more loathsome than the clutch of his hand on her hair. She smelt his breath on her skin, sour with vicarious erotic excitement.

With a great burst of adrenaline, Julia pulled away. There was a sickening sting of pain as a plug of scalp tore free. She staggered, dropping her phone. She righted herself and thundered back along the corridor, her elbows striking the wall in panic.

Footsteps pounded after her, the labored breath frantic, the clatter of the shears maddening. She reached the front door. He was on her again. Another crunch as a lump of hair left her head. She yelled for help, her voice pulling blood from her throat.

The front door swung open. Screaming and fighting his hands away, Julia tumbled into Marie's arms.

"Julia!" Marie said. "Calm down. Whatever's the matter?"

"He's here. The tondeur. The shearer," Julia said, staring into the blackness of the house behind her.

"There's no one here," Marie said, steadying her and grasping her hands. "We're in the house on the other side of the street."

"The women. They're back there, in the courtyard."

"No, they're not. We're all over there."

As Marie led her away, Julia stared back at the house. The clicking had started again. It was following them, bouncing off the walls of the cobbled street and swirling ahead through the mist to the house on the other side.

Unplaced in category

LITTLE SALLY SHARPE

Genre: Thriller • **Theme:** An interception • **Character:** An alumnus

Inappropriate behaviour in an Oxford College results in a fitting retribution.

The phone was startlingly loud in the rarefied atmosphere. Cursing, Sal Sharpe fumbled with the receiver. "Professor Osborne's rooms." She listened. "Oh, Ron. Thank goodness it's you."

"You're out of time," the college porter said.

"I've barely finished making the bed."

"He's dining at Balliol College. He'll be back by eleven."

"Can't you delay him?"

"You're more likely to succeed than me. Let me finish up."

She clattered down the stairs and met Ron coming across the Quad. Handing over the master key, she said, "You could lose your job for this."

The college porter sagely shook his head. "I've looked after Mordiford students for over thirty years. I'm not stopping now."

"I'm not a student anymore."

"Makes no difference to me, miss. You've answered the call."

Sal looked up at the clock tower on the other side of the Quad, its face glowing like a moon in the summer twilight. "You've got your phone?"

Ron nodded, patting the breast pocket of his blazer before tipping his bowler and setting off towards the Senior Common Room, working the master key back onto the bunch in his fist.

Sal went out into the street. Despite the hour there was a waft of balminess in the air, and the promise of a hotter day tomorrow. The streets teemed with students, young and vital, pouring out of bars and chatting around tables. She remembered feeling like them, and she remembered having it ripped away from her.

Then she saw him, Professor Osbourne, striding down Mordiford Lane, his college gown boiling blackly behind him, the clip of his steel-capped brogues echoing a snappy tattoo around the ancient walls. She turned away, pressing a hand momentarily onto the wall as she steadied herself and texted, "He's coming."

She moved into deeper shadows. The click of the heels increased in volume. She stared at the ticks on her phone. Grey. Still grey. Ron hadn't read the message.

Someone called out, "Good evening, Prof," as she touched the telephone symbol to make the call, but before it even connected, a body barrelled into her back, sending her and the phone flying. It skittered away from her fingertips, coming to rest against the foot of the college steps. "Damn and blast," she said, retrieving it and running a thumbnail across the shattered face.

"Well, if it isn't little Sally Sharpe."

He was every bit as tall as she remembered, but his once plentiful hair had thinned on either side of his forehead, accentuating his peaked hairline.

"Professor Osbourne," she replied weakly, rising to her feet.

A grin spread across his large features. "I only just recognised you." He stepped back a pace, appraising her. "Your hair is so short. You look sophisticated, gamine somehow. I remember you as being a bit…"

"Lumpy?"

"That's harsh – well-covered I'd say. What are you doing with yourself these days?"

"Working for justice."

"The law!" he chuckled. "I can't say I'm surprised. I seem to remember you liked carrying the odd banner or two in the past, and you certainly had the brain. If I'd been your tutor, you would have got a First."

"I did get a First."

He pushed his hands deep into the pockets of his trousers, rocking back on his heels. "That was tactless of me." He gave a self-deprecating laugh. "Let me make up for it and stand you a nightcap, for old times' sake?" Before she could answer, he took her by the elbow and ushered her gently up the steps into the college. Passing the Porter's Lodge, he released his grip and peered in. "No Ron tonight? You must remember Ron," but Sal had stepped out into the Quad was looking up at the second floor.

The lights were still on. The Hitchcockian shadow of a

man in a bowler hat moved across the pane like a magic lantern show. She stared down at her dead phone, her mind racing. Was it possible that Ron was about to finish the search? Or that the professor would be so engaged in conversation with her that he wouldn't notice the lights were on in his rooms? She couldn't risk it.

"I remember a fabulous little bar in the High," she said, sliding a friendly arm through Osborne's and drawing him back towards the open door.

"I assure that I've got a very fine whisky up in my rooms."

"Maybe later," she said, smiling up at him, squeezing his arm as they weaved their way through the crowds.

"Those tattoos must raise a few eyebrows in Court?" he said as they walked.

"The justice system isn't like it used to be."

He flashed an arch look at her. "And I bet those robes cover a multitude of sins."

The fabulous little bar in the High, of course, had changed. A wall of lights flashed epileptically, the music numbingly loud. "There's a quieter pub down Grape Lane," he shouted, his breath warm on her ear and scented with wine.

"Or we could have that whisky," she shouted back, certain that Ron would be finished now. The sooner she steered the professor back to Mordiford College, the sooner she could wind things up and be gone.

"Don't fancy a stroll down Grope Lane, then?" he said darkly.

"I beg your pardon?"

"That's what it was called back in the thirteenth century. A hundred years earlier, it was called something far cruder, using an acronym I wouldn't dream of uttering in these delicate times, but it rhymes with..."

"Thank you. I can guess."

"Not sure you can."

"I'll look it up."

"I bet you will," he said, leaning forward with a raised eyebrow, a canny look sliding into his eye. "My rooms it is then."

"EVENING, SIR," Ron said, looking up from his newspaper as they passed the Lodge.

"Evening, Ron. All quiet?" the professor said. "You remember Ms Sharpe?" he added indicating Sal.

Ron narrowed his eyes and peered out. "Can't say I do, miss. Hard to remember every face that passes by the Lodge over the years." When the professor turned away, Ron gave Sal a barely perceptible nod.

As Osbourne prepared the drinks, Sal affected an intense interest in the bookshelves, whereas in fact she was making certain that Ron had completed everything that was needed. Osborne indicated the sofa with practised ease, clinked the lip of his glass against hers and sank back, his arm draped behind her.

"Your good health, little Sally Sharpe."

"It's not Sally."

"No?"

"Sal is short for Salome."

The corner of his mouth lifted approvingly. "You naughty little girl."

She took a sip of whisky, the alcohol burning down her throat, pulling down her chin. The springs beneath them creaked as he leant across, relieving her of her glass before coming in for the kill.

This time Sal was ready, this time she had a plan. Despite the clink of his teeth against hers, the sucking mouth and the searching hand, she slipped cat-like away and moved towards the bedroom door. He watched her in some surprise, his breathing rapid, his face flushed. "Goodness. You've certainly matured since last time. Know what you want now, huh?"

"Oh, yes," she said, undoing her top button.

He padded towards her like a panther, his hands working away at the belt of his trousers. When he reached her, she slid his belt away, drawing him towards the bed and pushing him back onto it with a playful but powerful shove.

As he fell backwards, that ludicrous smile of baffled intrigue was still on his face, but the instant his full weight hit the mattress, he arched his back, his eyes wide with horror, his hands flying to his stomach.

Prone now, he raised his head, watching with horror as blood bubbled between his fingers and a spring of thick metal spiralled up from his diaphragm. With shuddering fortitude, he took his hands away from his body, tucked in his chin and pressed himself upwards, a terrible bellow forcing itself from between his teeth as the spring reversed, disappearing agonisingly back into his body.

He was up, his face distorted with savage rage. She felt the same terror that had paralysed her so effectively in this very room a decade ago, a shameful failure to save herself, to fight, to flee, but before he reached her, he coughed, sank to his knees, and toppled forward like a felled tree.

She drained her whisky and rinsed the glass, placing it back on the tray. Ron was waiting in the Porter's Lodge. He handed her an envelope. "It's all in there," he said. "Every complaint against him, every gagging order, every piece of evidence."

"Nothing to suggest this was anything other than a dreadful accident."

"That antique furniture would never pass health and

safety standards these days. By the way," Ron added. "The Home Bursar at Pembroke College has a situation over there. It could do with your decisive touch."

UNPLACED IN CATEGORY

BITE

Genre: Suspense • **Theme:** A DNA test • **Character:** A grocer

When estate agent Nigel Henshaw takes a bite out of one of her husband's apples, Karen Babbage sees a perfect opportunity to change their lives for the better.

Nigel Henshaw looks completely out of place in Babbage's. He's prowling around the shelves on the other side of the potato sacks, the trousers of his cheap suit sticking out below his preposterous padded jacket. The only other customer in the shop is Mrs Crow, picking out eight Brussels sprouts for Sunday lunch. Henshaw pushes past her, snatches up an apple from the tilted display basket and sinks his portcullis crowns into the flesh.

When he reaches the counter, he's still chewing.

"It's freezing in here," he says, "How do you stand it?"

"Years of practice," I say, my arms wrapped tightly round my body.

He drops the half-eaten apple onto the counter and leans forward.

"It really is time to move on, love. Have a word with your husband. You won't get a better offer.'

Angus struggles through from the stock room carrying a crate of leeks, sees Henshaw and drops them to the floor. Mrs Crow jerks her head up like a spooked horse.

"What the hell are you doing here again?" Angus says, thundering across the shop towards Henshaw, "You can't keep harassing us like this. It's unethical. How many times do we have to say no before you damned well leave us alone?" He pushed his face into Henshaw's and said, "We're not interested."

Henshaw has the good grace to step back a couple of paces but then he points at me and says, "I bet your wife's interested. Look at her, shuddering away behind the counter. Her lips are blue. This ramshackle collections of sheds and outhouses needs burning down to the ground."

"How dare you."

"And trade isn't exactly booming, is it?"

As if to underline his observation, Mrs Crow shuffles up to the counter with her handful of sprouts and places them on the scales.

"That'll be 22 pence, Mrs Crow," I say quietly. "Shall I put them straight in your basket?"

"Yes, please, dear."

After she's gone Angus turns back to Henshaw.

"Babbage's has been in my family for three generations," he says. "No amount of money is going to make me turn my back on the business or the village."

"With the option I'm offering you, you can start up somewhere else. Nice little shop on the high street maybe, passing trade…"

I don't much like Henshaw but I know the man's right. I can picture the four gorgeous little houses a developer could build here; I wouldn't mind one myself. It's not that Angus and I aren't good at business; it's the location, stuck down a muddy lane at the edge of the village. No one knows we're here, apart from the locals. I said to Angus only the other day,

"Putting 'Buy Your Cabbages from Babbage's' on the side of your van isn't going to cut the mustard unless you use it to drive around and woo the local pubs and restaurants."

But he's a stubborn Scot and as long as Babbage's still stands, my life will never change.

Their discussion is getting heated now. Angus bangs the counter so hard that the abandoned apple gives a little bounce. It gives me an idea. I can solve all our problems and get rid of this odious estate agent at the same time. I welly in.

"You heard what my husband said," I shout. Both men turn to me, astonished. I never raise my voice. I come out from behind the counter and shove Henshaw hard on the shoulder. "Get out of here, and don't bother coming back."

Henshaw shakes his head, a sly smile lifting the corner of his mouth as he backs away.

"Whatever's got into you, Karen?" Angus says as Henshaw heads towards his car. "You've never been on my side about this before."

"He can't come strolling in here, helping himself to things." And with that I snatch up the apple with my gloved hand, step out of the shop and fling it with all my might at Henshaw's car. It hits the windscreen with a bang before bouncing up into the air and disappearing into the long grass of the verge.

Henshaw holds up his hands in mock surrender, gets into his car and drives away.

"Well, Karen," Angus says, joining me at the open door. "I always thought you couldn't wait for me to sell up."

I kiss him on his bristly cheek, link my arm through his and give it a squeeze. He thinks he knows what's best for us, but he's wrong and there's only one way to show him. I need to sort this out myself.

When Angus goes back to the stock shed, I take a paper bag outside and hunt along the verge for the apple. To be doubly sure, I fold the bag over my glove hand, retrieve the apple without touching it and take my treasure round the back of the sheds, tucking it out of sight underneath a wooden pallet. When work finishes for the day, I retrieve it, wrap it tightly in plastic before taking it home and tucking it away at the back of our freezer.

I double check that our insurance is up to date and, while I'm at it, I go over the sums. It looks like we'll get at least £700,000 from the insurance, which makes Henshaw's offer of £200,000 a complete insult. I know exactly what he'd do if he got his sticky hands on Babbage's. Knock the place down and sell the land to a developer for four times as much, which is exactly what I plan to do now that I have a scapegoat in my sights.

It takes me a few days to get everything organised. I top up the petrol can when I'm filling the van and tuck the can away behind the shop where we chuck out the empty cardboard boxes. When Angus is closing up, I work out of sight, stacking the cardboard against the wooden cladding of the building until I've built quite a nice little pyre. Finally, everything is ready.

We don't live over the shop; our house is a few hundred yards further down the lane and once Angus is flat on his back, snoring at the ceiling, I slip out of bed, grab my clothes off the chair and creep into the bathroom to dress. Downstairs, I retrieve the frozen apple. By the time the police take it away for DNA testing, it'll be thawed and fresh as the day it was bitten.

There's no moon tonight but I have no trouble navigating the familiar terrain around the property. I make my way round the back of the sheds so that I don't trigger the security light. Once I'm behind the shop, I feel around in the dark for the can.

I hear the security light come on with a click, like the snap of a rubber band. My heart, which was already bouncing around in my chest, seems to stop altogether before careering off in another direction. I strain to see if I can catch the sound of footsteps. All I can hear is an owl in the spinney on the other side of the paddock and the wind lifting the tress along the perimeter fence. I creep along in the shadows until the front of the shop is in sight. Nothing. No one.

Then I see it – the scuttling black shape of a large rat hurrying across the car park. He must have set off the security light. I pat my chest to soothe my heart before making my way back. I pour the petrol onto the cardboard pyre, being careful not to splash my clothing. I light a match. I toss it into the boxes.

They burst into flame with such a mighty whoosh that I leap back. I cast an anxious eye at our house on the other side of the fence. No light has come on; Angus is still asleep. One more task to complete.

As the flames trickle up the wooden cladding, I retrieve the apple from my pocket, imagine where Henshaw would stand to watch the flames and lay it gently onto the grass.

All is quiet when I let myself into the house. I wash my hand carefully, sniffing them to make sure that the tang of petrol has gone. I undress and carefully climb into bed next to Angus. He stops snoring, stirs and rolls over towards me, gathering me up against him. By now, I can see the red glow on the ceiling of the bedroom. I wait a little longer. No point going to all this trouble only to have Angus call the Fire Brigade in time. When I heard the crackle of fire and a soft crump of falling beams in the distance, I shake him awake, panic in my voice.

"Angus. Wake up! Someone's set fire to the shop," and with a snort he springs upright like a jack-in-the-box, staring wildly around the room. Then he bounds to the window.

"Good God," he says, "Call the Fire Brigade, Karen. The whole place is ablaze," and he's struggling into his clothes and clattering down the stairs.

I don't call the Fire Brigade, not straight away. I watch from the sitting room window as Angus paces up and down, sometimes running forward then retreating, his hands on his head then raised to heaven. I feel a dreadful pang of sadness for him, but I know all will be well in the end.

It takes the Fire Brigade ages to arrive and then they can only get one engine up the lane. They spray the remains of the smoking buildings until steam pours into the cool air of dawn.

The following days are filled with people. There's a steady stream of villagers, some coming to gawp, others to drop off cards of condolence. The fire investigator comes. He says it's arson. The police are sympathetic and kind. I make them tea. I want to say, "And the apple? Did you find the apple?"

As the days pass, anxiety swells inside me. When I see the police putting a tent around the spot where the storehouse stood, I feel as if my innards are rebelling, my stomach churning. I can bear the suspense no longer.

I walk across and ask what's going on. I'm told to go back to the house. There's something about the gravity of the constable's voice, or the look he gives me which makes fear rise in my chest like nausea, sour and unstoppable. When the officer knocks on the door half an hour later, I jump. Angus looks at me and frowns.

He goes to the door. The officer comes down to the kitchen and I stand. Finally he says the words I've been longing to hear.

"We've found a match to the DNA at the scene of the crime," he says.

I can almost feel the bones of my chest easing as the tension pours out of me.

"The apple?" I say and Angus and the officer look at me.

"I'm afraid all the stock has gone, madam," the officer says. He turns to Angus again. "Do you know a man called Nigel Henshaw?"

"Indeed we do," Angus says. "He's been trying to get our shop off us for years. Are you telling me that he set the fire?"

"It seems the most likely explanation."

"Has he been arrested?" I say.

The officer turns to me, his expression grave.

"Arrested? No. His body was so badly charred, the only way we could identify him was testing his DNA against his sister's."

"What on earth was he doing inside the shop?" I say.

Angus and the officer stare at me, frowning and I feel myself beginning to blush in that scalding, incriminating way.

"He was setting the fire," the officer says. He narrows his eyes. "Is there something you'd like to tell me, Mrs Babbage?"

"No, officer," I say. "Nothing at all."

Honourable mention in category

WHAT A TALE YOUR THOUGHTS COULD TELL

Genre: Sci-Fi • **Theme:** Greathearted • **Character:** A caregiver

A husband is certain his wife resents his disability and there may just be a way to find out.

Jamie swam languorously in the warm current of the chalk stream, navigating between the mats of floating flowers, glistening like stars on the river weed beneath the harsh light of high summer. He kicked out into the middle of the river where the flow was stronger but the water colder, replenished by springs bubbling up from the aquifers deep in the earth. As he rounded a bend in the river, he saw Stella sitting on a bank of shingle. She rose to receive him, towel in hand, her face a blank of mute irritation. He didn't kick for the shore, he imagined floating on past her, on and on until he reached the ocean.

There was a click as the technician released the headset, a hum as the couch slowly elevated Jamie into an upright position. Jamie stared down at his legs, once tanned, defined, strong – now thin, pale, and utterly useless.

"Stop it, Jamie," George said with mock severity. Jamie smiled and gave a guilty chuckle. He liked George. He guessed they were roughly the same age, thirty-something, although George's liquid crystal contacts gave his eyes a somewhat owlish appearance, making him seem older. George placed the Lecta tablet back in its dock and raised a quizzical eyebrow. "I wouldn't have done it," Jamie said. "I wouldn't have floated on by but..."

George's eyes moved back to the tablet as the screen glowed orange. "But you thought about it."

Jamie gave a dismissive puff. "You know I thought about it, but can't you see that I wouldn't have done it?"

"Not unless you think it." George picked up the tablet and turned the face towards Jamie. "And you didn't think it. You imagined floating out to sea. You come to the respite centre to escape from that type of thinking." George smiled indulgently. "Come on, it's nearly lunchtime. I'll take you over early."

As George prepared the electric scooter, Jamie gazed at the Lecta, the colours changing in harmony with his thoughts, the lines of text – his thoughts expressed as words – flowing and correcting as his mind jumped between concepts. If only he could borrow it, just for one evening ...

The Lecta pulsed a gentle warning tone. George retrieved it, glanced at the most recent line of text, and turned it off. With a sigh he sat down. "I really shouldn't let you do that," he said.

"I'm sorry. It's just if I knew for certain what Stella thought, I wouldn't need to imagine floating out to sea."

"But what if the Lecta confirmed your darkest fears?"

Jamie felt a flip deep inside his abdomen as if his pod had suddenly dropped onto a lower rail. "You've always told me they're unfounded, that Stella doesn't resent having an invalid as a husband."

"Because I don't think she does. She works hard to enable you to be here during the working week, and when she comes to collect you, she seems genuinely delighted to see you."

"It's not natural."

"What isn't?"

"She wasn't like that when we first married. She's become more – I don't know – demonstrative than she used to be."

"But that's wonderful, isn't it?"

"She's covering something up. I'm certain of it."

George drew across a chair and sat, resting an ankle on the opposite knee. "As a species we're very bad at reading other people's thoughts. Before the invention of the Lecta, even the most perceptive people only got it right sixty percent of the time."

"Sixty percent? That can't be true."

"That's what the research shows. It's rather comical if you think about it. We're a highly sociable species and understanding what other people think of us is essential if we want to stay in the safety of the tribe. Yet, after three hundred thousand years of practice, we get it wrong forty percent of the time, and thank goodness we do. Imagine a Lecta app on your phone. It'd be the end of society as we know it."

"Rubbish. If the Free Thought lobby had their own way, it would be available now."

George rolled his lips between his teeth, a habit of his when he was thinking. "When you had your accident," he said at last, "did you want to know what the people who found you were thinking? As they worked to get you out of the wreckage, would you like to have known that the man with the laser cutter was thinking about…" George puffed and waved a hand around in the air, conjuring an image, "what he was having for tea; or know that his assistant was reliving the sex he had the night before?"

Jamie pulled a disgusted face and was quiet. He was glad George had turned off the Lecta. He didn't want him to see the waves of intense irritation running through him, anger at this greathearted man who selflessly devoted his time to making life tolerable.

"The negative thoughts are getting stronger," Jamie said. "I'm only free from them when I'm journeying with the perception headset and they're strong enough to overpower that at times."

"And I'm here to bring you back when they do. I tell you what, I'll book you in with the Alpha Centre and we can recalibrate the headset."

"It's been recalibrated three times already. Knowing what Stella's thinking is what I need to sort me out."

George peered thoughtfully at Jamie. "When I was a child and Lecta seemed as impossible as jumping into a new time zone, my grandmother gave me some very good advice."

"Which was?"

"Never ask a question unless you are prepared for both answers."

"So you *do* think Stella resents me."

"This has nothing to do with what I think." George leaned forward, splaying his hands across his knees. "What if, for the sake of argument, you lock the Lecta onto her beta waves at the very moment an uncharitable thought flashes through her mind – just as it did for you a minute ago?"

"What on earth are you talking about?" Jamie threw a glance at the Lecta, checking it was definitely off.

George followed his glance and chuckled quietly. "The Lecta has taught me to trust my instincts, Jamie, and I could tell by that narrowing of your eyes and the hardening at the corners of your mouth that you were irritated with me."

"I was, just for a moment, but I'm in purgatory, George. Won't you make an exception, just this once?"

George checked over his shoulder although he must have known no one could hear them. "I'll be in the most dreadful trouble if it ever gets out."

"It won't. I promise you. I'll be forever in your debt."

"And you understand the risk you're taking?"

"Absolutely."

IT WAS one of those rare English summer evenings when the heat of the day still lingered despite the setting of the sun. Jamie sat outside on the terrace, watching Stella in the lighted window of the kitchen, handing the dirty plates to the assistant before shutting it down for the night. He felt a shameful thrill from observing her without her knowledge. She pushed a flop of hair from her eyes and gazed sightlessly out towards where he sat in the dusk, although he knew she could not see him from the lighted room.

The Lecta lay on his lap, inert and black, obscured by the table at which he sat. Stella had lit a candle and was coming out of the door. His fingers felt along the edge of the tablet, searching for the switch to power it up.

Cupping the flame with her hand, she lowered it to the table, lightening her face. She widened her eyes at him and gave him the warmest of smiles. He glanced down at his lap where the Lecta lay, still dark, still lifeless.

Just then the clear song of a blackbird rang out from the thicket of trees at the bottom of the yard. "Oh," Stella breathed. "How beautiful. He's singing his heart out." She took up her glass and held it out for a toast. "He's bidding farewell to the weakening light. Here's to us," and she tapped the edge of her glass ringingly against Jamie's.

His heart beat so fiercely, he was astonished that she

couldn't hear it, but she had kicked away her shoes and stretched back, looking out across the yard, her head tipped attentively to one side as she listened to the trilling song.

The urge was almost unbearable. If he turned it on now he'd know, once and for all that she loved him. A feeling of shame crept over him, stronger than when he watched her in the lighted window. His body felt packed with sweat. He looked across at his wife, innocent and unsuspecting, secure in the knowledge that she was doing the best for him, for them. And yet… and yet…

"On an evening like this," she said softly, "isn't it just wonderful to be alive?"

Unplaced in category

FEEDBACK EXAMPLE

WHAT THE JUDGES LIKED ABOUT YOUR STORY

Judge 2089

Thank you for submitting What a Tale Your Thoughts Could Tell *to the Short Story Challenge 3rd Round. This is an emotionally intelligent and unexpected sci-fi short story featuring unique sci-fi ideas and relatable technology, a complex debate at its core, and important, relatable, and distinct characters. There's a lot to like here—I think you've tackled sci-fi from a new angle, providing an emotionally diverse drama that discusses technology, disability, and relationships in a very original and new way. No aliens, robots, or spaceships to be seen—instead, grounded and 'real' storytelling, using the science-fiction genre as a lens to discuss hypotheticals and genuine human issues. The Lecta app is especially well-utilised, feeling analogous of something that exists, or could exist, in our own world. This is definitely a stand-out piece of writing, using the genre in a fresh way, and presenting us with a keen drama. I hope it takes you far! It's clear you have an original voice as a writer.*

Judge 2076

Something that struck me in your writing was how rich your descriptions were, using such varied and original sensory detail. Even in the first paragraph you've got the 'warm current', the 'floating flowers' that glint like stars, the 'bubbling' springs–it's stunning, and what's more you maintain it throughout. Great work!

Judge 1689

Marvelous opening as Jamie imagines allowing himself to float away from his wife Stella–only to have George–the tech monitoring his thoughts with the help of Lecta–call him out for that kind of thinking (because that is what he is precisely there to work on). Strong scene as Jamie stubbornly insists that the only thing that will rid him of these negative thoughts is to discover how Stella really feels: nice touch that he distrusts her because she is more demonstrative than she used to be–all of that creates a terrible sense of foreboding for George and for us. Powerful turn when George lets Jamie take it home–and he finds himself struggling with the urge to turn it on even as Stella shares her heart with him.

WHAT THE JUDGES FEEL NEEDS WORK

Judge 2089

Firstly, I think your opening sentence is over long—running onto three lines—and could be simplified. For instance, the clause 'glistening...' may not be crucial to our understanding. Be clear, be concise, be direct, and if we don't need a detail, remove it so we can focus more closely on the story itself. Think about this throughout—it's also a good idea to read your work aloud. This is a good way to adjust your narrative flow, ensure your sentences don't feel overlong, and that your story is being communicated clearly and concisely. 'Stop it, Jamie'–Stop what? This section doesn't feel clear. I think 'Stop it' should come after 'He didn't kick for shore'—these ideas are connected. Then, 'There was a click...' Again, think about how you're communicating your story and how it flows together. Take a look at Pg. 3 and 4—both rely very heavily on dialogue, and I'd prefer some narrative variation—keep describing, reacting, emoting, and observing. Keep the narrative engaging—especially in dialogue and exposition-heavy sections. Good luck with your future development!

Judge 2076
What could be a point to develop in this piece is your ending. As mentioned there's this amazing description in this piece but the final image is quite brief, and I wanted to linger for longer on the images of his beloved wife against the backdrop of the peaceful setting, and I wondered whether you could cut words earlier–perhaps cut some of the dialogue in the second to last section–to make space to linger longer on this final image, really leave your reader with the kind of memorable image that your wonderful piece deserves.

Judge 1689
Gorgeous characters and premise. As you explore the suggestions below, hold onto your approach and characters as they are working well. Also, though it is quite complete as a short, I would love to see you develop this into a novel. For now, however, let your story develop more quickly. Though I love the exchanges between George and Jamie, I would love

to see you spend more–and maybe even most of your time with Jamie and Stella. The idea that our thoughts don't tell us more than our actions and choices is really powerful. Equally powerful is the idea that our guilt and worry can lead us to believe almost anything and take actions that we know are going to end in disaster. Let Jamie take definitive action. Turn on Lecta or refuse to. Show us what happens next. Is he freed of his obsession or not? Does he find a way to be honest with her? Does she find out? Does she feel betrayed? Is she working at being there for Jamie so that it is hard and different? Or did his injury soften her heart toward him? You have raised all of these wonderful questions. I think you can make the time to answer them if you trust your core premise and let Jamie have the Lecta by the middle of the story or perhaps even earlier. Good start. Keep working on it. Good luck!

ASSIGNMENTS

2018: Round 1

Genre: Action/Adventure • **Subject:** A rite of passage • **Character:** An apprentice

2500 words in 8 days or less

Chapter 3: **The Butcher's Boy's Bicycle**

2018: Round 2

Genre: Suspense • **Theme:** A DNA test • **Character:** A grocer

2000 words in 3 days or less

Chapter 13: **Bite**

2019: Round 1

Genre: Thriller • **Theme:** Exile • **Character:** A philanderer

2500 words in 8 days or less

Chapter 10: **A Dish Served Hot**

2019: Round 2

Genre: Horror • **Theme:** A rental • **Character:** A hairdresser

2000 words in 3 days or less

Chapter 11: **The Tondeur of Marseille**

2020: Round 1

Genre: Comedy • **Theme**: An exchange of gifts • **Character**: A nosy neighbour

2500 words in 8 days or less

Chapter 1: **Blown Away**

2020: Round 2

Genre: Spy • **Theme:** An award ceremony • **Character:** A welder

2000 words in 3 days or less

Chapter 7: **Careless Talk**

2021: Round 1

Genre: Drama • **Theme**: Mainstream • **Character**: An influencer

2500 words in 8 days or less

Chapter 5: **Germany Calling**

2021: Round 2

Genre: Romantic Comedy • **Theme:** A lapse in judgement • **Character:** An ambulance chaser

2000 words in 3 days or less

Chapter 6: **The Slow Burning Fuse**

2022: Round 1

Genre: Ghost Story • **Theme:** A silent auction • **Character:** A loiterer

2500 words in 8 days or less

Chapter 2: The Shivering Ladder

2022: Round 2

Genre: Suspense • **Theme:** A seminar • **Character:** A recreationist
2000 words in 3 days or less
Chapter 8: **The Stone Circle**

2022: Round 3
Genre: Thriller • **Theme:** An interception • **Character:** An alumnus
1500 words in 2 days
Chapter 12: **Little Sally Sharpe**

2023: Round 1
Genre: Political Satire • **Theme:** Contractual obligation • **Character:** A do-gooder
2500 words in 8 days or less
Chapter 4: **Spirit of the North**

2023: Round 2
Genre: Romantic Comedy • **Theme:** Loyalty • **Character:** A rhythmist
2000 words in 3 days or less
Chapter 9: **The Bodhrán**

2023: Round 3
Genre: Sci-Fi • **Theme:** Greathearted • **Character:** A caregiver
1500 words in 2 days
Chapter 14: **What a Tale Your Thoughts Could Tell**

ACKNOWLEDGEMENTS

My biggest debt of gratitude has to go to everyone at NYC Midnight. Writing these stories has taught me to think on my feet, to tackle genres I wouldn't have touched in the past (sci-fi, political satire) as well as inspiring scenes that I later amended and included in my novels.

I would like in particular to thank Nikita Andester for responding positively to the idea of this anthology. As writers we are so used to publishers, agents and companies saying "no", it was a breath of fresh air when Nikita came back with an enthusiastic "yes"– but with this group of people, I shouldn't really have been surprised. As she said in her email, "NYC Midnight genuinely cares about the writers and how they grow from the competitions," and her support of this project underlines this powerfully.

I'd like to thank writer friends who have joined me in some years, getting different assignments, sharing their stories and feedback with me, in particular Isobel Brown, Amanda Edwards-Day, Mandy Robotham and Howard Teece.

My biggest debt of gratitude goes to my family – Chris Truby for his patient beta-reading and constant encouragement; and my children Sam Fergusson, Ben Fergusson and Katie-Jane Whitlock for shutting me in my writing room and taking over the catering one Easter Sunday when an assignment inconveniently arrived on the same day as the family.

BOOKS BY THE AUTHOR

Writing as Loraine Fergusson

The Duntisbourne Hall Mysteries

The Archivist
The Golden Hand
The Hipkiss File

Writing as LP Fergusson

A Dangerous Act of Kindness
The Summer Fields

The Archivist is none other than BS Moreton, one of the stars of the short story Blown Away. If you enjoyed him blundering into a heap of trouble on the river bank, you'll certainly enjoy reading about his ludicrous tumble from grace in this full-length novel.

If you enjoyed the humiliation of Hector Schofield in The Slow Burning Fuse, you can meet him again as he continues to pursue Max's love interest in this full-length novel.

Major Frodsham and BS Moreton's antics on the river bank in Blown Away inspired a whole section of plot in the full-length novel, The Hipkiss File.

Printed in Great Britain
by Amazon

38395538R00076